"Listen!" Crowbar snapped. The throaty clunk of an oar hitting stone sounded above the roar of the river.

Joe stared into the darkness. The water was only a shade lighter than the canyon walls, and the waves slightly more pale. Joe squinted at a crest. It darkened before his eyes, then lightened. "Someone just went past," he said, his fear beginning to mount.

"Yeah," agreed Crowbar. "And at night. Man, that's heavy. Think someone's after us?"

. . . Joe unsnapped his life jacket from the tall cedar bush where he had secured it for the day to keep the strong canyon winds from blowing it into the river.

"Did you tell anyone about this job?" Crowbar asked.

"Come on," snorted Joe. "Think I'd tell anyone about this?" He gestured toward the small coffinlike casket on the bottom of the raft. "I won't even tell myself about it. I just say to myself we're having fun riding the river at night. You and me . . . best friends stuff."

# RIVER RATS
### INC.
by
## Jean Craighead George

**Vagabond Books**

SCHOLASTIC BOOK SERVICES
New York Toronto London Auckland Sydney Tokyo

*To River Rat,*
*Margaret Craighead*

ISBN 0–590–32118–8

12 11 10 9 8 7 6 5 4 3 2 1        1        3 4 5 6 7/8

# RIVER RATS,
## INC.

# CONTENTS

# The Beach

Joe Zero awoke to the drum roll of 83-Mile Rapid. He pushed to his elbows and listened. The dam, he thought, the dam upriver across the Grand Canyon has broken. In the dark reddish light of twilight he looked for an escape route.

Sheer walls hemmed the plunging river on both sides, and above these, cliffs and mesas formed mountain steps a mile into the sky. Rocks, ramparts, and a vast hot silence surrounded him. There was no way out but on down the river.

The drum roll crescendoed and he dashed the few feet to the water. By the river's edge, 83-Mile Rapid hummed more quietly, and he saw that the water had actually dropped a few feet. The daily rise and fall marked the use of water at the power plant upriver at Glen Canyon Dam. Joe blew a breath of relief, then wondered what he had heard.

Putting his ear near his sleeping spot he realized the rock against which he had lain, together with the cooling of the evening air, had amplified the

1

sound of the rapid. He laughed nervously at the deceit. The Colorado River, dangerous at its best during the daytime, was by moonlight, as he was now forced to travel it, downright perilous. He needed no terrifying tricks of nature.

A coyote barked to his mate from a high plateau where the sun still shone, and into the darkness of the inner canyon came piping bats. They flew and tumbled like autumn leaves. Comforted by their living presence in the soulless rockscape, Joe shook his friend who was sleeping under a pile of drift-wood.

"Hey, Crowbar," he said. "It's almost night. The moon will soon be up."

It was time to continue their strange and dangerous trip.

Joe pulled their inflatable neoprene raft out from under the bushes where he had hidden it so that it would not be seen from the river or the air during the day. He and Crowbar had no permit to run the Colorado, so they floated by moonlight to keep out of sight of day-running parties and primarily of the National Park Service that patrolled the river by daylight.

As Joe picked up his oars his eyes fell on the casket lashed to the bottom of the raft. He shivered.

"Some deal," he said aloud, then forced himself to forget the gruesome job he and Crowbar had accepted three days ago.

Joe tested one oar on his thigh. Last night he had heard it crack in Grapevine Rapid as he rowed the turbulent water, facing downstream in the manner of river runners. Grapevine was a roaring maniac of a falls. It had spun their small craft like a karate expert, and had snapped his oar when he fought back.

The crack was not as bad as he thought. Opening

a waterproof metal box, he took out a roll of plastic tape, wrapped the stem, and tested it once more. It was firm and strong.

He unsnapped the metal food locker and took out a jar of peanut butter and a box of crackers, then walked over to Crowbar.

The sun dropped out of sight. The sky turned purple. Two planets appeared and brightened swiftly. Night comes suddenly on the Colorado.

He squinted and gazed out at the watery path. He knew the river well; he and his Uncle Como had run it many times, but not at night. Moonlight made the Colorado a beast with wet claws that clutched, and watery teeth that snapped and swallowed boats.

"Crowbar. Wake up!"

Crowbar grumbled. He should have been named Bearbar. He was more sleeping bear than early-rising crow. When awake, however, Crowbar was a piston — quick, precise, and bold. Joe admired these qualities, for he himself was fearful and slow to catch on to things.

"Get up!" he shouted to his friend. Crowbar peered out from under the logs and blinked.

"Where am I?" He saw Joe. "Oh, yes, with you, in hell." Crowbar grinned and his small white teeth flashed in his dirty, sunburned face. Knocking the sand off his cheek, he crept out from under the brush.

"No copters, huh?" he asked, then glanced at the river. "Anyone out there?"

"Nobody but us would be so dumb at this time of day," Joe replied.

Crowbar shook the sand out of his shoulder-length black hair, then relieved himself on the driftwood and sat down. Joe passed him the peanut butter and crackers. A quarter moon came over the wall of the canyon and illuminated the roaring water.

3

"We're four miles above Phantom Ranch and the suspension bridge," said Joe. "We've got to sneak past the area. The Smokey Bear Feds hang out there."

"Ummm," mumbled Crowbar.

"There'll be a lot of campers just beyond the bridge. That's where the Bright Angel trails come down from the North and South Rims."

"Where's Phantom Ranch?"

"About a half mile from the river. If we hug the north wall we'll be out of sight of it; but it's really no problem. Everybody's singing and eating there."

"The campers? Do you think they'll see us?"

"They're going to be a problem."

"Guess we better leave the camouflage on the raft tonight."

"Yeah, and add some more."

Joe pulled the raft halfway into the water. Crowbar handed him a fresh salt cedar branch and he lashed it to a pontoon.

"How did we get into this anyway?" Joe asked.

"Your Uncle Como got us into this," Crowbar snapped. "*He* got us the job."

"Yeah, but this night stuff. You said there is a five-hundred-dollar fine and/or six months in jail for running the river without a permit."

"*I* was trying to get us out of the deal; then *you* said we could run it at night and keep out of sight."

"Well, what else could I say? You wanted the job, too. . . . All that money . . . besides, the old lady didn't want any National Park fuzz messing around with her mission." Joe waded into the icy river and filled a plastic bottle with muddy drinking water. He added a few drops of Clorox to purify it and tied the jug to a ring on the bottom of the raft so it would not bounce out.

4

"This is our third job as president and vice-president of Dirty Work, Inc.." said Crowbar, lashing down another salt cedar branch.

"And it may be our last, if we aren't careful. Pull something over the casket. Those brass bands shine in the dark," said Joe.

Crowbar, wiping his perspiring face with his arm, streaked his long straight nose and wedge-shaped chin with mud.

"I sure didn't think we'd have so many lousy jobs when we went into business," he said. "That was awful collecting that money from the cowboy at Tompkins Ranch."

"Shooting the sick dog was worse," said Joe. "I hated that."

"*This* is worse," said Crowbar, pointing to the casket. "But two hundred bucks and all expenses paid ain't hay." He fastened the food locker, an army surplus ammunition box that had two latches and lids which effectively sealed out water.

"And I thought Dirty Work, Inc., meant washing windows and cleaning attics," sighed Joe.

"Maybe this *is* dirty work," mused Crowbar.

"Naw, the old lady was okay, just nutty. Lots of nuts come to Las Vegas. All you have to do is watch TV. The gambling and the nightclubs attract them." Joe said.

"Listen!" Crowbar snapped. The throaty clunk of an oar hitting stone sounded above the roar of the river.

Joe stared into the darkness. The water was only a shade lighter than the canyon walls, and the waves slightly more pale. Joe squinted at the crest. It darkened before his eyes, then lightened.

"Someone just went past," he said, his fear beginning to mount.

"Yeah," agreed Crowbar. "And at night. Man, that's heavy. Think someone's after us?"

"Maybe the Havasupai Indians have some night-rafting ceremony," Joe suggested hopefully. "Know of any?"

"Me? My family hasn't lived in the canyon for two generations. I'm about as much Havasupai as you are Greek or whatever you are. What are you?"

"I don't know. . . ." Nervously he licked his lips and tried to concentrate on his parents and grand-parents. "Western," he said finally. "We're western mix, a western omelet."

Crowbar, still staring at the river, managed a laugh. "Me, too, a dozen eggs, a little green pepper, some onions, and some tomatoes . . ." His voice trailed off as he leaned down to get his paddle. "But let me tell you something, Western Omelet: I think we're being followed."

Joe unsnapped his life jacket from the tall cedar bush where he had secured it for the day to keep the strong canyon winds from blowing it into the river.

"Did you tell anyone about this job?" Crowbar asked.

"Come on," snorted Joe. "Think I'd tell anyone about *this*?" He gestured toward the small coffinlike casket on the bottom of the raft. "I won't even tell myself about it. I just say to myself we're having fun riding the river at night. You and me . . . best friends stuff."

Crowbar checked the ties on the back of Joe's life jacket. then turned around so Joe could check his. "They're tight," Joe said, jerking them to be sure. He climbed into the boat.

Crowbar took his position in the front, on his knees, with the important "trouble-averting" paddle.

Joe pushed the craft off the beach, crawled into the semi-rear, faced downstream, and pushing hard on his oars, steered into the main current.

The river grabbed the boat and swept it swiftly toward 83-Mile Rapid.

# The Suspension Bridge

The voice of 83-Mile Rapid rose from a drum roll to the thunder of a detonation. Joe stood up and studied the water. The first big rapid was ahead. The test of his skill was imminent.

Eighty-three miles from the put-in, Lee's Ferry, he thought. One hundred and fifty-two miles of rapids to go. He sat, sculled, and steered the raft into the current. He must keep it in the center of that speeding vortex to ride out the boil without capsizing.

The last time he had been down the river was in May, a month before graduating from junior high. Discouraged by his poor grades he had taken a job as cook with a rafting outfit and had quit school for two blissful weeks on the river.

At the end of that run he came whistling home to Uncle Como, with whom he had been batching it in a trailer since his mother had remarried shortly after his father's death. That night over a pizza dinner he told his uncle he would like to become a professional river rat.

"Why not?" Uncle Como had said quickly. "The river's an education in itself."

The next day when Joe repeated Uncle Como's words to Crowbar, he, as usual, leaped two thinking bounds forward.

"The river's an education?" he said. "Well, then, we ought to quit junior high and get on with our doctoral degrees. I saw in the paper where River Float, Inc., is hiring cooks and boatmen." That afternoon they applied for jobs.

All would have gone well had not Mrs. Flood, Crowbar's mother, answered the telephone when the offers came in. She took the message, and was waiting when Joe came by to pick up Crowbar for school. As Crowbar came out of his room she glared from one to the other.

"Do you think you're going to get away with this?" she asked. "Taking jobs before school's out. Do you know you have two more weeks and three more years to go? Now give me an explanation."

Crowbar repeated Uncle Como's wisdom about the river, and Mrs. Flood swished through the door and strode down the block to the trailer. She found Uncle Como sipping coffee and reading the paper.

"Do you realize you're encouraging those boys to drop out of school?" she hissed. "They've got jobs on the river."

Uncle Como laughed pleasantly. "They'll learn a business," he said. "What could be more virtuous and American than becoming businessmen?"

"Businessmen," she snorted. "My eye. They're playing hooky and you know it. When they become businessmen they can leave school with my blessing." With that, she walked out, head high, nostrils tense. Snapping her heels, she escorted Joe and Crowbar down the street to the school-bus stop, and there she stood guard until they were aboard and on their way to school.

Inside, Joe hunched down in the seat, embarrassed and defeated.

"Well," said Crowbar brightly.

"Well what?"

"Well, let's become businessmen."

Joe slowly turned his gaze upon his friend, grinned, chuckled, and then burst into laughter. "Okay," he said. "Let's."

That afternoon they asked their social studies teacher if they could do an independent study on the small businesses in Las Vegas. Surprised and delighted by their sudden interest in school, she agreed, and after class they went to the courthouse to register a new business — Dirty Work, Inc. The following day they placed a small advertisement in the Las Vegas newspaper. Then they waited.

The days passed, no jobs came their way, and graduation from junior high was suddenly upon them. Mrs. Flood escorted them to the function. The speaker was a local advertising man who lectured on how to be a success in the business world. Crowbar leaned over to Joe: "What we need is a catchy advertising campaign."

The following morning Joe drew a dollar bill with a bloody arrow piercing it, and lettered:

**LET US DO YOUR DIRTY WORK.**
**Call Dirty Work, Inc., 487-4211.**

They duplicated two hundred copies and spent the next few days slipping them into local mailboxes and under the room doors in the big gambling hotels.

10

Three days later they had their first two jobs, but after collecting the money and shooting the sick old dog, they decided they'd rather go to school. Then the phone rang and Uncle Como told them to go to Room 1278 at Cleopatra's Palace, the casino-nightclub on the neon-lit gambling strip. The next thing Joe knew they were hauling the casket to the raft.

Joe shook the memory out of his head and concentrated on the river. 83-Mile Rapid rumbled ominously, and again he got to his feet. Peering through the darkness he saw before him a cauldron of gray foam into which a tongue of slick water jetted. He steered to the center of the tongue that was the signature of deep water between two rocks, then lifted his oars. He was on mark.

The water sucked them into the rapid. They dragonflied up a crest, hovered on the top, and dropped, it seemed, into the belly of the river. Joe heard the clink and thud of stones rolling on the bottom. He was listening to the creation of the canyon: water, sand, and rocks carving and cutting the land.

They climbed a tall wave, fell, climbed another, then slid like a skater across a smooth area into a hole. One side of the raft was sucked down by a whirlpool. Water poured in and filled the boat instantly. Still buoyant on its inflated tubes, it spun twice, roller-coastered over a line of small waves, and was shot out into calm water. They were through 83-Mile Rapid, their first big one.

Joe whistled softly and bailed out the water.

"Good run!" Crowbar whooped.

Joe felt his shoulders straighten and his head lifted with pride. "Now for the suspension bridge and the

Smokey Bear fuzz," he said matter-of-factly, and dug in his oars.

The bridge loomed into view with suddenness. Flashlights twinkled along its span as backpackers crossed in the night. Below it campfires glowed peacefully. Then Joe saw a figure with a wide-brimmed hat. "Ranger on the bridge." He pulled branches over him. "Get down under the spinach!" he said and hunkered down.

"You ain't going to steer?"

"No! Get down!"

Crowbar vanished.

The raft twisted in the current and drifted toward the middle of the bridge. Two late backpackers met the ranger and stopped to talk.

The bottom of the bridge spun overhead as the raft wheeled under the basketry of steel girders and cables. The stars reappeared and they were out from under the bridge and in full view of the hikers and ranger if they looked down. Through the branches Joe saw them talking animatedly. So involved were they in each other that they did not notice the dark mass below that was brush, raft, Joe, and Crowbar.

Joe hoped they had lots to say as, with painful slowness, the raft drifted downriver. At last it rounded the bend and they were out of sight of the bridge.

"Phew," he breathed and pushed back the branches to find that they were almost beached on the hikers' campground. Voices and laughter rose on the night air, singers hummed in harmony, guitars strummed, and everyone, it appeared, was pre-occupied with evening pleasures.

Then Joe felt the river runner's nightmare. They were going upstream. Caught in an eddy they were doomed to circle endlessly unless he could pull them across the eddy fence, a two-way street of fast water. One strong pull at the top of the eddy was needed to bring them out of this; but the movement must be the right one, at precisely the correct time. Joe unlocked an oar.

The raft drifted upstream past a cluster of campers gathered around a fire arguing over who should clean the pots. So heated was the discussion that they did not see the brush-covered raft not five feet away.

Joe sneaked his body along the pontoon and was raising an oar to dig into the water and pull them across the eddy fence when two children suddenly appeared in the darkness. They ran to the beach, scooped up water in buckets, and threw it at each other. Joe swore softly. He had to pull right now and risk being discovered. He took the chance, stood up and pulled.

The boat quivered, moved out, then spun and was sucked back into the eddy.

"Lie low," Joe called. "We're going around again."

The campers had resolved their argument. One grumbling girl was at the river's edge washing the pans. She did not look up as the raft passed her in the darkness. Joe listened for the children as they swung toward the top of the eddy. Not hearing them he crept up and sat on his seat. He pulled on both oars with all his might. The locks clunked as he went over the eddy fence. He was sure the entire campground heard, but no one called out and no one looked up. The current grabbed the raft and sped them downriver into the shadows. Joe sighed and listened to the river mumble.

"Close call," he said.

They were still soaking wet from 83-Mile Rapid, and when a cold wind created by the rapid ahead blew upriver, they both began to shiver. Joe opened

13

the tool locker and took out wool sweaters which they pulled over their wet clothes after removing their life jackets. The fabric and the preservers held in their body heat and presently they were warm. They leaned back and drifted under the moon's enchanting light.

But no sooner were they comfortable than they were swept around a sharp bend and saw, on a wide beach, a large party of people who were floating with a commercial outfit. The boatmen of these outfits were skilled rivermen, Joe knew. Their trained eyes would see the difference between driftwood and a branch-covered raft. They also kept the rules of the river. If they discovered Crowbar and him floating without a permit, they would probably turn them in. The five-hundred-dollar fine flashed before Joe's eyes.

"Keep down," he whispered to Crowbar, then groaned. They had struck the edge of another eddy. Not daring to row, Joe waited as they rode to within a few feet of the beach but stayed on the outside of the fence. Two boatmen at the river's edge filled their water bottles without looking up, and Joe wiped the perspiration from his neck as they drifted safely past.

A few minutes later he thanked the stars. Before him was only a pie-shaped wedge of night sky between the black walls of the canyon.

"Okay," he called to Crowbar. "We're safe. This is the Inner Gorge. No one will be camping here. There're no beaches for miles and miles—just sheer walls and water. Neat place."

For the next several hours they drifted in silence.

Joe could hear Crowbar's breath coming gently as he watched the stars and dreamed.

Beaching the raft before dawn, Joe opened a box

14

of cereal and handed Crowbar a dish. They were quietly eating when the *clap-clap* of a helicopter blatted out.

"The fuzz," Joe said, lay down and covered himself with sand. Crowbar tunneled into the sand and both lay still. Only their eyes and noses were uncovered.

In moments they were looking up at the glassy belly of the park whirlybird. It swung and dipped like a hornet, hovered above them, then clattered on.

# The Casket

Three nights later the three-quarter moon illuminated the current line so well that Joe steered almost easily through Serpentine and Waltenberg Rapids, fast good ones. He needed only to hit the current dead center and the water shot them right down. The trip was fun at last. Joe felt he was handling the rapids well, and with Crowbar's strength on the forward paddle, they floated swiftly through the inner walls of the awesome canyon.

Upon reaching Elves Chasm and seeing that no one was camped there, Joe beached the raft.

"There's a beautiful spot up in this side canyon," he said. "Flowers, ferns, clear warm water. Let's live it up."

Snapping their life jackets to a tree, they ran up a boulder-filled stream to a cascade that dropped fifty feet into a bright, clear pool. With a hoot Joe took off his sweater and splashed into the crystal water fully clothed. He surfaced, called to Crowbar, and together they swam and dove. Pulling up into the shallows they washed the river mud out of their hair and off their clothes and bodies. Then they drank the good pure water spilling from the rocks and filled their bottles.

"In the daylight this water is a beautiful green," Joe said and glanced at the top of the canyon. He blinked. For an instant he thought he saw someone run along the rim but upon a second glance he saw nothing. His imagination was running away with him.

When they were clean and refreshed the boys boarded the raft and hit the next four rapids with skill and abandonment.

On the quiet stretches between the rough water, Joe let Crowbar row, and the miles slipped by. They passed one motor launch and one oar boat party; then the walls steepened into a long stretch with no beaches. The canyon was theirs. Walls polished by the water to glasslike slipperiness rose straight out of the river. They relaxed and drifted.

"This is living," said Crowbar, putting his feet up on the bow and leaning back on one of the two pontoons that lay across the boat.

"Hey, there's that boat again," said Joe. He pointed. "Over there against that white wall."

"Yeah." Crowbar sat up straight. "Think he's following us?"

"Why should anyone follow us?"

"The Feds?"

"Naw, they'd roar up in a motor launch. This guy is sneaking down the river. He's always along the edges."

"Hey," whispered Crowbar, "someone's crawling out of that eddy or, at best, a piece of someone . . . big, a tilted head."

"I'm . . ." gulped Joe, "scared crisp . . . crisp as that guy in the box."

The current gathered speed and they sailed around a bend and on deeper into the canyon.

The other boat did not follow, but now that the subject of their mission had been brought up, both boys thought about the casket.

"Wonder what it's like to be dead?" Crowbar finally asked.

"Man, I'm going to know if that boat turns up again. It really scares me to death."

The deep voice of a big rapid sounded ahead.

"Dubendorff," said Joe. "This one's a boat-eater. Gobbled up an oar boat twice the size of this thing last summer. It got caught in a keeper and the water just ripped it to shreds, although the people got out okay. Let's dock and look at it. Maybe we'd better rope down this one."

Joe put the raft into a cove and leaped out on a shore of water-tumbled boulders. Climbing to the top of the highest rock he studied the falls in the coming of dawn's light. Waves leaped fourteen feet into the air, broke into muddy spray and snarled around dark rocks.

"Let's rope her," he called. "I've had enough excitement for one night."

Crowbar took the end of the coil of rope tied to the nose of the raft, and Joe kicked the boat. It swirled away. Crowbar fed out the line, as he ran adroitly over the boulders, following the bouncing raft as it plunged through the rapid. Presently he called: "She's down," and Joe scrambled over the rocks to join him. "No one is going to camp on this beach," he said. "Let's quit for the day." Joe looked around. The landscape was as rocky as the moon.

Crowbar brought out a wedge of cheese and a loaf of bread, then sat down against a boulder.

"There he is again," Joe whispered, pointing to

the nose of a pontoon boat roaring up on a Dubendorff wave. It rode the big crest like a chip, then plunged out of sight. At the end of the rapid the craft shot into view once more, then vanished in the misty dawn light.

"What do you make of it?" Joe nervously wiped his mouth with the back of his hand.

"Don't know."

"Think we're in trouble?"

"Maybe this guy," he gestured toward the casket, "didn't die?"

"Didn't die? What do you mean?"

"I mean, suppose he was murdered."

"Murdered! Wow, man, that's heavy."

"We're getting paid a lot of money."

"Yeah." Crowbar shook his head thoughtfully. "Yeah, we are."

Downriver in the weeds and brush, the bell-like voice of a canyon wren signaled the rise of the sun. Joe smiled and welcomed the cheerful sound. Crowbar, however, was hunched into a silence deeper than the black hole of space.

Finally he cleared his throat and straightened his spine. "I'm going over every step of that meeting in the hotel room. There's something fishy about all this. Maybe you're right about this job." He closed his eyes and began.

"You and I are knocking on the door of Room 1278. A butler or somebody like that opens it; anyway, he's in uniform and he takes us into a suite. Then your Uncle Como comes in smiling and glad to see us. He slaps you on the back and escorts us into a darkened room."

"Yeah," interrupted Joe. "He *was* glad to see us, wasn't he? . . . *Real* glad."

"Red velvet drapes are pulled across the window

19

and when my eyes adjust to the gloom I see an elderly woman sitting in a big leather chair.

"The lady has a handkerchief and she dabs her eyes.

"Now your uncle Como speaks: 'Mrs. Streeter,' he says. addressing her, 'these are the young businessmen I was telling you about.' She nods and dabs her nose. He turns to us.

"'Boys, Mrs. Streeter's husband, Mr. Roland Streeter, died recently. He loved the Colorado River and so in his will he requested that his ashes be dropped over Lava Falls. Would you like to do the job?'

"You nod and I say: 'What about a permit? There's a five-hundred-dollar fine and/or six months in jail if you are caught without one.'

"Then you say: 'We won't get caught if we run it at night.' Your uncle Como says that's a swell idea and the old lady dabs her eyes and nods real fast.

"I say it's pretty dangerous to run the river by day much less by night, so the butler or whoever he is says: 'Would two hundred dollars make the trip safer?' Stunned by that news I say: 'Yeah.' Then the butler says: 'We want proof that Mrs. Streeter's job is done. How will you prove it?'

"Next thing your Uncle Como takes a camera out of his pocket and says: 'Joe, snap a picture of Crowbar tossing the urn that's inside the box.' He turns to Mrs. Streeter: 'I know every wave in Lava Falls. No picture, no money.'

"Then I say: 'Isn't it dangerous to scatter ashes when you're going over Lava?'

"And Uncle Como says quickly, 'No scattering! I don't want your lives endangered. Throw the whole urn. Hear me? No scattering. Now listen to me, Joe. Go over the falls by day. Lava's a deathtrap if you don't hit it right. Wait along the shore until dawn when you can see.'

"Now," said Crowbar, back in the present, "is there anything wrong with all that? There *is* an urn, we checked it at Lee's Ferry."

"Just one more thing, Crowbar," Joe said grinning sheepishly. "What does *naive* mean?"

"Naive means you're kind of simple and innocent. Why?"

"Well . . ." Joe shuffled his feet. "As we were leaving I heard the butler ask Uncle Como if there might be any complications and he answered: 'Never, Joe's as naive as a field of daisies.' "

"Ummm," said Crowbar, "that's not so good." He thought a minute. "But your uncle wouldn't get us messed up in anything bad. He's a nifty guy."

"Yeah," said Joe with pride. "He really is."

The sun struck the wall of rock behind them and the blue purple shadows of dawn exploded into gold.

# The Night Rider

In the late afternoon a river party passed down Dubendorff Rapid, awakening Joe with hoots and hollers. He peered from behind his rock to see two people in a raft with supplies, and four in kayaks, the slender little Eskimo-style boats. In one of them was a young girl. She hit a hole in the rapid, spun up on end and turned over. After a long instant she rolled her boat back up and sped on down the river, paddle flashing, her laughter a tinkle on the boom of roaring water.

Joe whistled in admiration. To roll the kayak took skill and guts. He would like to meet that girl. Kayakers were the aces of the Colorado River. Alone in their tiny boats with double-blade paddles, these people could skim, dive, run upstream, roll, and dart. He longed to be one of them but did not have the nerve or the stamina.

Uncle Como had tried to teach him how to paddle and roll a kayak, but in the practice lessons in a swimming pool, he had been so frightened with his head hanging down under water that he could not think how to right himself. He had squirmed out of the boat and swum for the pool's edge.

His mother was right. He *was* the family misfit. His oldest brother, Ed, was a football end and an honor student, and his kid brother, Sam, was a runner-up in the statewide diving competition. He, too, got high grades in school. But not him, Joe. He was an athletic, scholastic disaster.

When the kayakers had skimmed away, Joe watched the river flow in lazy swirls that set him to daydreaming.

He was running the Colorado standing up in a kayak. Leaning into the waves he steered by bending his knees and skimming like a surfboarder. He climbed, dipped, turned, upset, and rolled up again. His mother was clapping. She did not care that he had flunked math and English, and when he beached she asked him to leave Uncle Como and come back and live with her. She missed him very much, she said. Joe lifted his dream kayak over his head and told her he would think about it.

He had gone to live with his Uncle Como because he and his mother had fought and bickered almost constantly since she had remarried. His stepfather was the vice-president of a bank, and when Joe's grades went down, she became upset.

"You're never going to get anywhere if you don't apply yourself like your brothers do," she said one night.

"I do. I am trying hard," he screamed at her. "I just can't learn. I don't understand algebra or the books I have to read."

One night he asked her what Charles Dickens's *David Copperfield* was all about. She was peeling potatoes in the kitchen sink. Slamming down the food she spun on her heel. "Sam and Ed didn't have any trouble with that book," she snapped, "but then they *read* it. They didn't come bawling around asking what it means."

That did it. Joe covered his head with his hands.

"I'm leaving. I'm no good anyway. Uncle Como asked me to live with him. I think I will."

She did not answer. He waited for her to beg him not to, but she kept on peeling potatoes.

That night Joe packed up and moved into the trailer with Uncle Como.

Life with his mother's brother, a construction engineer, turned out to be a mind-boggling treat. When out of work, he took Joe down the Colorado, taught him to stalk and hunt game, and once they had flown over the Grand Canyon with a pilot friend of Uncle Como's. As they had looked down on the vast chasm, they had agreed that even glittering Las Vegas was a mud puddle compared to the colorful three-hundred-mile long and twenty-mile wide canyon the river had made.

While at Uncle Como's, Joe had learned to cook. Since his uncle was often gone for days, he taught himself to make bread, barbecued beef, and curried chicken. He also figured out how to bake pizzas, and deep-dish apple and blueberry pies. Occasionally in the evenings he looked at his uncle's geology and history books on the Grand Canyon, and memorized the names of rapids, campsites, and rocks, for he wanted to know the river as well as his uncle did. He knew not only the rapids, but the eddies and the footpaths down to them. But when Joe closed the books at night, he felt the task he set for himself was as discouraging as school. He was a slow learner.

When the chef job with the raft outfit came up, Joe took a cooking test, passed well, and was given the job. He had two blissful weeks on his own.

Joe stopped dreaming. His long shadow foretold the end of the day. He awakened Crowbar. In a few minutes they were out on the muddy river.

The moonlight transformed the giant rock blocks into massive temples through which they wound on a watery highway. Joe raised his voice in song and Crowbar joined in.

"Too bad old Roland is cramped down in his little jar and can't see all this beauty," Joe said when the song ended.

"You wonder why a guy wants to be dumped down here," Crowbar said. "He'll be just a speck in all this rock and dirt."

"Maybe that's why he did it. Maybe he felt like a speck."

A dying fire on the shore illuminated the four kayakers, and the girl came back to Joe's mind. He steered close to shore. No one stirred. They were all asleep.

A satellite wheeled across the sky. Crowbar pointed it out.

"I'd like to work with those things someday," he said.

"Man, you really got to be bright to do that kind of work."

"I could do it," Crowbar said. Joe nodded. That was the thing he liked about Crowbar. He had confidence. He *could* do it.

Joe, facing downstream as river rats must do to see where they are going, rowed swiftly, setting a fast cadence for Crowbar, and they sped through miles

25

of quiet water. The cliffs along the river receded and were replaced by great deltas that were the mouths of ancient rivers.

After a long pull, Joe beached the raft about a mile above Havasu Canyon, the popular rafting stop. The sun popped over the cliffs like a fireball, and the day dawned hot.

"Let's find some shade," Joe suggested.

The food locker slung between them, they walked through a narrow canyon of sandstone for almost a mile.

The walled stream bed led to a bright spurt of water that shot out of a rock, pooled, and seeped off underground. They did not need to vote on this site. Both flopped down by the pool and rested in the shade of the cliff.

"Someone's coming," Joe blurted. "Look! The red ants. They're scattering."

Crowbar did not wait for a lecture on ant behavior. He shoved the food locker under a rock, grabbed the wall, and scaled it.

Joe followed him to a ledge where they lay down on their bellies.

"Those canyon red ants used to walk in gangs and bite campers," whispered Joe. "They can really hurt, so outfitters and river rats sprayed them with chemicals, stepped on them, and threw hot coals on them. After a while the ants learned to be more clever. Now when they feel a human footstep on the sand, they spread out and hide. When the people depart, the ants come back and pick up the garbage."

"Ssh," said Crowbar.

Steps sounded on the gravel of the canyon floor. A small boy dashed into view. He was naked, his movements agile and catlike. Long matted hair fell over his shoulders. The skin on his thin body was cracked and rough like a dog's paw. He made no sound.

Suddenly he leaped on a lizard and stuffed it into his mouth. Beneath his dusty hair, large deep-set eyes gazed blankly as if he were in a trance.

Then a lizard moved and his eyes came alive. He snatched it.

Stalking and hunting, the boy came upon Joe's and Crowbar's wet sneaker prints on the rocks. He started, sniffed the air, then raced down the canyon corridor, leaping in long, deerlike bounds. At the bend he swung to a ledge, climbed a hundred feet to the rim, and vanished, a blur in the hot light.

"What was *that*?" gasped Joe.

"I wonder if he's our night rider," Crowbar said. "He's weird enough."

Joe whistled softly. "He's been living out here a long time. See his skin? Takes a lot of wear to get that many callouses."

"Well, he can't hurt us. Didn't even have a knife," said Crowbar. "Lucky kid, leaping around and living wild and free in these pretty canyons."

"Yeah, and eating lizards. No thanks."

Joe rolled over on his back and closed his eyes to sleep for the day. A rock dug into his hip. He removed it and lay back again. He tried to relax, but could not. Visions of the wild boy zoomed around his head.

"Our boat," gasped Crowbar. "You don't think he'd take it?"

Without answering, Joe threw his leg over the cliff, let himself down. Crowbar followed. Each grabbed a side of the locker, and they sprinted to the beach. The boat was still there.

"Where's your oar?" yelled Crowbar. "One's gone. He took it."

"Geez," said Joe. "I can't go over Lava Falls with one oar. We've got to catch him."

They jumped aboard just as the sound of the park helicopter blatted far upriver. Out they plunged, pulled the raft into the reeds, and looked around for cover.

"Where do we hide? The reeds won't do." Joe saw a mud hole left by the falling river and jumped into it. Rolling over and over he caked himself with wet clay. Crowbar did likewise. Then they both lay still, peering up out of the puddle, slimy-bodied and white-eyed. The rangers looked right down on them without a flicker of recognition and passed on.

When the helicopter was gone the boys crawled out of the ooze looking like prehistoric tadpoles. Seeing each other they burst into roars of laughter, then jumped in the river and washed off.

"Man, what a mud battle we could have," shouted Crowbar.

"No time for horseplay," said Joe. "The copter's gone for the day. Let's find that oar."

Shoving the raft into the river again. Joe used his one remaining oar as a paddle. They shot two small rapids, then paddled hard down a long flat stretch.

Just before they reached Havasu Canyon Joe spotted the wild boy's pontoonlike boat jammed in an eddy. Crossing the river by angling on the current, he pulled up beside it. It was a single pontoon, one of a pair that are strapped together to a wooden platform to make the big oar rafts. Worn and beaten, it appeared to be the remains of a wreck.

"He must ride the thing bareback, hanging on to the straps," said Crowbar, studying the tube. "There's no other place to sit."

"How could he? His feet would go numb in that water."

"I don't know, but I do know your oar's not here."

"Look!" exclaimed Joe. "The Lizard Boy's on that wall." He was hopping like a goat down the ledges, listing slightly to one side, a burlap bag over his shoulder. Joe recognized it as one of the beer bags that the outfitters tie to the rear of their rafts to keep their passengers' beer cold. In rough water these often broke loose and floated away.

"Hey, kid!" shouted Crowbar. The boy did not look up. "Seen my oar?" The tousled head did not turn at the call.

"He can't hear," said Joe. "His face is a blank."

Suddenly the dull eyes lit up and the boy jumped into the eddy and snatched a floating orange. He stuffed it into his mouth with one hand, clutched a bag of potato chips with the other, and after swallowing, ate it, paper and all.

"Man, he survives on the stuff in the eddies," said Crowbar, scratching his head, "and lizards."

"Smart kid," said Joe. "Eddies are the supermarkets of the river. Everything ends up here: food, sleeping bags, boat parts. Hey, that gives me an idea. Backwater, Crowbar."

The boat turned, and Joe angled it out into the current and crossed the river to the opposite wall. Sensing what Joe was up to now, Crowbar stood and scanned an eddy along the bank.

"There it is!" he shouted joyfully. "Your oar! Caught in an eddy."

Joe drew hard to the left. Crowbar reached out, grabbed the oar, and kissed it with a smack.

"Well, deaf and dumb Lizard Boy taught us something," he said. "How to use eddies. That was too close for comfort." He paused. "I wonder how the oar got in the river."

"I tossed it on the beach earlier this morning," said Joe, shaking his head, "and forgot to tie it to the raft. The river rose while we were gone. Dumb of me, man. That was real trouble."

Joe rowed; Crowbar paddled in silence for the few minutes it took to pass Havasu Creek.

"Ever go to Supai, the Indian village?" Joe asked.

"Once. My father took me when I was about five."

"Beautiful place," mused Joe. "I climbed up from the river one time. I was really impressed by those blue-green waterfalls, the gardens, and that avenue of huge cottonwood trees. And the way the only transportation is racehorses and burros. Must be a neat place to live."

"I don't remember," said Crowbar. "I just wanted to get out of there the day I went. Dad drove the highway department caterpillar then, and all I could think about was going home. He promised to let me sit in the cab if I went down to Supai with him."

The rocks around them suddenly changed. They became black and shiny like long cannon barrels piled one upon the other, aimed down at the raft.

"Crystallized lava," Joe explained when Crowbar objected to their appearance. "We're inside an ancient volcano. It erupted about a billion years ago and dammed up the river. One night the dam burst, and all that is left is . . ."

"Lava Falls," answered Crowbar.

Domes of other volcanoes were lumped across the landscape; clouds cast blue shadows across them, and only a few strange plants grew on their slopes.

"Eerie down here," said Crowbar.

"Yeah," agreed Joe. Then cold wind struck them, rippling the yellow surface of the river.

"That's the wind from Lava Falls," said Joe, swallowing hard. "We're about a mile from it. Let's

30

quit and spend the rest of the day and the night along here. Uncle Como wants us to go over at dawn."

There were no beaches, so Joe steered toward a slick wall of water-polished lava. He tied the raft to the downstream side of projecting rock, and sliding down into the bottom of the raft opened the food locker. They were under a huge overhang. No helicopter could see them.

"We sleep aboard ship," he said.

# Lava Falls

Joe could not sleep. After twitching and turning he sat up, tied the food locker more securely to the rings on the floor of the raft, tested his life jacket, and looked over the map of the river. Lava Falls was the granddaddy of all the U.S. rapids. Joe closed his eyes and tried to recall how Uncle Como had entered it. At a considerable angle so that the current would straighten the raft.

"Crowbar," he said, "let's get out of here. I'd like to beach near the falls and have a look at it. The Feds are gone and no one's coming."

Crowbar sat up.

"Have you steered it before?" he asked.

"No." Joe's nostrils flared as he tried to calm his voice. "I want to look at that hydraulic, the keeper at the bottom of the first drop."

Crowbar needed to hear no more. He picked up

his paddle, kneeled in the front and, when Joe untied
the raft, went to work.

They beached on black stones behind a rock buttress
where a few sprays of desert grass eked out a tough
living in the cinders. Joe jumped out.

"Tie her up," he called, and took a well-trodden
path that led to a lookout rock above the falls. Many
river runners had walked here before, to do precisely
what he was about the do . . . read the mood of
Lava Falls.

The noon sun turned the clouds above the black
lava hills orange and pink. A raven flew overhead
checking to see if Joe had food. He shooed him
away and licked his dry lips.

"Suppose I don't hit the slick at the right angle,"
he said to himself, then wiped the thought from his
mind. "I've got to. I will."

His and Crowbar's lives were at stake. Perspiration
pooled at the base of his neck and suddenly he was
thinking about his father. He had been a sheriff in
Las Vegas, a brawny man with a wide, toothy smile,
who understood little boys and helped them to keep
out of just such trouble. Joe recalled the day his
father discouraged him from climbing out on a tree's
dead limb. The next day his father was killed in a
street fight. From that day on, Joe's life began
spinning down into crazy whirlpools.

Suddenly tears were pouring from his eyes. Glanc-
ing around to make sure he was alone, he dropped
to his belly and cried as he had never cried before.
He had hoped to accomplish so much on this trip:
prove that he could do something worthwhile, finish
an assignment, use his head in emergencies, be the
person he wished he were. Now he was scared. He

knew he could not run the falls. His father would have prevented him from taking this impossible trip.

When the tears had stopped flowing and had dried into salty patches on the hot rock, he pushed up on his elbow. Lava Falls thundered on and on. Scrambling to his feet, Joe dashed to the lookout. The boiling water tumbled and danced down the falls, sending splatters of mud high into the air.

The boat-eating "keeper" lay to the left of a big boulder that jutted out into the river on the north bank. The right side of the tongue dropped into it. That left side, however, flowed smoothly away from the hydraulics. His course should be down the tongue precisely one foot to the left of the middle. He wheeled and ran down the path. He could do it.

When Joe got back to the raft, Crowbar was eating sardines and cold spaghetti, both of which he offered Joe.

"I'm not hungry. Think I'll pass up the feast," he said.

"Well now, what do you know," said Crowbar, pointing. "Here comes Lizard Boy."

The youngster was clambering down the steep wall of rock shelves, his toes grabbing like fingers as he plunged from one stone to the next. At the water's edge he leaped lightly into their raft, snatched the half-eaten can of spaghetti and finished it off. Before Joe could stop him he had wolfed down the sardines and grabbed an apple out of the open food locker. Biting it in half, he swallowed it without chewing.

"Get out of here!" yelled Crowbar. The boy stuffed the other apple half into his mouth and reached for a box of raisins.

"Stop!" Joe shouted at the top of his voice. The boy did not even turn his head.

"He's deaf," said Joe, then roared to test him. He did not flinch.

"He doesn't see either," said Crowbar. "At least not us." He jabbed his fingers toward the boy's eyes. He did not even blink. Then he held up a chocolate bar. The child sniffed, focused his eyes, and grabbed it.

"He sure sees food," said Joe.

The sweet taste of the chocolate excited the boy and he pulled back his lips in a dog smile. One front tooth was broken, the others were dark but well formed.

Sniffing the air like a hound dog on a trail, Lizard Boy tracked another bar of candy to Joe's pocket. Amazed by this talent, Joe let him take it out. The boy squatted on the bottom of the raft and ate. His eyes met Joe's but it was as if Joe were not there, for he looked right through him. The boy shifted position to sniff out more chocolate, and his dusty hair parted on his back. Long scars reached from rump to shoulder.

"Wow, he's been beaten by someone," said Joe softly.

"Bet he ran away from home," said Crowbar. "Look at those old strap welts. Geez, I'd leave too."

When the boy's hunger was satisfied he leaped off the raft, ran on all fours up the slope, and wedged himself into a crack between two boulders. There he crouched, staring blankly at his feet. Then he lowered his head to his knees and in that position fell asleep.

"Wow! He's something," said Joe. "He seems to be all alone down here, living off lizards and eddies."

Joe and Crowbar watched the crooked little figure until there was no light to see by; then settling down in the bottom of the raft, they closed their eyes. This time Joe went right off to sleep.

The boy was still crouched above them as day dawned, but it was obvious he had already put in a day's work. In his hands was a lizard, and he was stuffing a small bird into his mouth. Crowbar tossed him a chocolate bar. He smelled it coming, reached out and snagged it with hawklike accuracy. He devoured it, paper and all.

"Man, he's quick."

"Hey, kid! Boy," Joe shouted. "What's your name?" The boy wiggled an ear to knock off a fly, but showed no sign of having heard. Joe reached for another candy bar. The wrapping rattled and the boy instantly stood up and focused on the candy. Then he darted forward.

"He not only sees and smells food, but he hears it," said Joe, tossing him the bar. "Imagine hearing food."

"He's sure not deaf," said Crowbar in awe.

Joe did not think about the Lizard Boy much longer. The sun was coming up over the horizon and there was a job to be done. Checking life jackets, the casket, securing the food locker and tool box, he and Crowbar readied the boat for the plunge. The park helicopter clattered overhead, but Joe had taken the precaution of lodging the raft behind the buttress in such a way that it could not be seen from upstream, and so he readied the raft without fear of detection.

Joe pushed out from the shore and Crowbar pulled on his paddle. The light was making stars out of the dew on the rocks and illuminating the black hole where the volcano blew. A bighorn ram looked down from a high rim. Ducks winged along the river, and the current swept them toward Lava Falls.

"Take five," said Joe, and Crowbar stopped paddling. The sound of Lava had changed from a growl to a roar. Joe opened the food locker, took out the camera, and placed it between his knees. Adjusting the raft with a backstroke he peered down the tongue of water.

"Okay, Crowbar, I'm on center. We've got to be a little more to the left and at more of an angle when we go over. Draw to the left until I yell stop. Then turn around. I'll hand you the urn. Toss it and I'll snap your picture. Got all that?"

"Yes."

Joe opened the casket. Inside, on dark purple velvet, lay a blue urn with a silver lid.

"Stop." Joe leaned out and handed the urn to Crowbar.

"Geez, it's durn heavy for ashes. Aren't you going to open it and scatter?" Crowbar asked.

"Uncle Como said to dump the whole thing . . . no strewing."

"But maybe Roland wants out," Crowbar chided.

"Hold it up for God's sake, Crowbar," Joe snapped. "We've got sixty seconds before we go over."

Crowbar held the urn over the water.

"Let her go!" Joe snapped the picture and threw the camera into the food locker. The latch jammed and he fumbled with it, swore, and then pulled on his oars. They were sliding to the right.

With a roar they shot down the tongue. The water sucked and hummed.

"Draw left!" screamed Joe. They slid downward, hitting the right edge of the hydraulic. Hissing waves hammered the raft and shoved it to the left. They worked like raging pistons. The raft trembled, came forward, halted, and moved backward.

"We're in it!" Joe yelled. "Stroke. Stroke. Stroke."

The right pontoon went under, the raft filled; then the churning water popped them forward.

"Pull! Pull!"

The raft moved backward and was hammered again by the thundering hydraulic.

"Once more! Pull!"

They moved out to the top of the boil, paddle and oars flailing uselessly in foam. Back they were towed by the water.

Joe glanced around helplessly. There was nothing to grab but waves. Then with a roar the water pounded the raft and a big bubble rose on the pontoon.

"This thing's going to bust. We got to get out," shouted Joe.

He opened the food locker, stuffed bacon bars and raisins in his shirt under his life jacket, and filled his pockets with candy.

"Grab the rope and jump as far out as you can when I yell," he shouted. "Don't swim. Get on your back, stick up your feet and ride the current. Don't fight it."

The raft moved to the forward edge of the keeper.

"Jump!"

Crowbar leaped, was suspended for an instant in an airwalk, then disappeared into the boiling mud foam. He came up, spun around, got on his back, and went down the chute out of sight.

The water pulled the boat back under the falls and pounded it. The pontoon ballooned and exploded with a scream. Balancing himself on what was left of the raft, Joe waited until he was at the downstream edge of the keeper; then he too leaped out as far as he could.

Under he went, up he shot, took a mouthful of air and glanced around. The keeper was behind him. He shouted, threw his feet up, and rode a fourteen-foot wave to its summit. There he hung for a moment, took a deep breath, and slid down into the boils and curls. He was pulled under, slapped in the face, and tossed onto the breast of another huge wave. He gulped air and muddy water and went under. Up he came, was carried buoyantly along on what seemed to be the top of a mountain. On its summit the waves juggled him like a Ping-Pong ball, and spidery rainbows flashed around him. And then he shot down a trough where he took a breath, and went under and popped up again. The waves were smaller now, and as he bobbed along he cheered aloud to the end of the roller coaster.

The rapids ended and the river ran smoothly. Joe saw the shoreline to his left and struck out for it. He grasped a rock, pulled himself ashore, flopped on his belly, and burped mud. Then, lifting his head, he scanned the river. One of the oars passed by on the main current, the toolbox spun up and went under again, the casket appeared and disappeared, but Crowbar was nowhere to be seen.

Joe watched. Minutes passed, one, two, three; no Crowbar. The raft, still in the keeper, was a mass of shredded neoprene.

"Joe! Joe!" came a frantic call. "Where are you?" Spinning around he saw Crowbar clambering up a nearby rock, dragging the rope behind him. Joe ran to him and threw his arms around him.

"Did you get the camera?" Crowbar asked when he had recovered from the shock of the water.

"Are you kidding? I got a little bit of food, that's all."

"Good-bye, two hundred dollars," said Crowbar, wiping his muddy cheek with the back of his hand. "Oh, well, I never did believe we were going to get that money."

As Joe realized they were both alive, a reaction set in and he began trembling from head to foot. Biting his lips, disgusted with himself, he sat down and put his head on his knees. The sun warmed him and the spasm slowly passed. Finally he sighed and looked at Crowbar.

"Now, what do we do?"

"Let's go down Lava again," said Crowbar. "I had a great ride." Joe did not laugh. Instead he shuddered and gazed out on the river in silence.

"The urn!" Crowbar exclaimed, pointing to a silver and blue object swirling buoyantly along an eddy fence. It rotated, bobbed up and down, then swung into the eddy and went out of sight.

"Good-bye, Roland," said Crowbar. "I hope you like it here."

"Don't you think its odd that it floats?" asked Joe.

Crowbar shrugged. "Who cares?"

In a short time their clothing dried in the desert sun and they walked upriver along the water's edge. Joe suggested they wait for a rafting party to pick them up. Crowbar reminded him that the boatmen would have to turn them over to the park fuzz.

"I'd rather walk out," he said. "If we can get to the top of that wall over there, it'll be all flat to Supai village. Probably only about twenty miles as the crow flies. They've got a telephone there."

Joe studied the grim walls of shale that rose above the lava rocks on which they stood. Heat waves shimmered off the rocks.

"It's hot on that wall. Maybe we could make it to

Supai if we find cans and bottles to carry water in. There's none up there as far as the eye can see."

He checked his jacket and shirt for the bacon bars. "We can eat okay for a few days. But water's going to be our problem." Joe checked his back pocket and felt his waterproof match container, bowie knife, and string.

"And we know lizards are edible," said Crowbar. "Let's go."

Crowbar jumped down to the river's edge and searched it for beer cans or bottles that might have been left high and dry as the water rose and fell. New Park Service regulations ordered that no garbage could be buried in the Grand Canyon, as once it had been. What was hauled in must be hauled out, so finding water containers was not easy. But Crowbar found a plastic Clorox bottle jammed under a rock ledge. He held it up, shouting triumphantly. just as Joe, rounding a boulder, spotted a bag of grapefruit in an eddy. He swam out to it and swung it around his head for Crowbar to see.

"That's worth our two hundred bucks," Joe called as he came ashore.

Peering under piles of driftwood for more cans, prying into fissures and crannies, they worked their way up the rocks along Lava Falls to a V in the wall carved by Prospect Creek. Here the stream reached the end of its journey down the side canyon and fell twenty feet to join the Colorado. Crowbar climbed up the side of the waterfall and entered a huge black bowl.

"Come up here," he shouted to Joe. "There's a pool, and reeds and rushes and birds!"

Joe joined him and they stood gratefully before a

41

blue pool that was lined with green plants. A frog croaked a single note.

"Hey, man, frogs. They're delicious," Joe said, cupped his hands and dove upon the singer. He held it up and Crowbar ran around to the opposite side of the pool. Using his T-shirt for a frog net he pounced upon the amphibians, and within an hour they had six large frogs.

"We'll make it to the village just fine," said Crowbar confidently. "We'll spend a day or so here catching enough stuff for the trip, and then take off."

A great blue heron walked out of a clump of willows, intent upon stalking fish. Crowbar lunged at it, but the bird took off when it sensed his mere intent.

While Joe skinned and prepared the frogs, Crowbar tried to chase a huge carp into the shallows. He finally cornered it under a rock, stuck his fingers in its gills, and held it up with a victorious whoop.

"That should last two days," yelled Joe excitedly, and he set out to find more water containers. He calculated that they needed about three gallons to get them across twenty miles of blazing hot desert land in the canyon.

Walking to the far end of the bowl he searched the ground in a circle spiraling inward, for he had read in one of Uncle Como's books that this site was a favorite campground for the river rats of bygone days. And *they* buried their garbage. One trash hole would probably have everything they needed in the way of containers.

His toe moved a rock and the tip of a rusted can showed. Excitedly he grabbed a flat stone and dug, uncovering a glass wine bottle and two one-gallon mayonnaise jars. Deeper in the pit was an old denim shirt. This he shredded into strips which he then braided into a long rope. Tying the jars together he slung the whole thing over his shoulder and had a water carrier.

He searched on, found another garbage hole and called Crowbar, who came running to see what he had found.

"Water jugs. We'll make it," Crowbar exclaimed and began digging.

A black phoebe bird, frightened by the boys, darted at Crowbar's head, but he paid her no attention. He had struck something.

"Aluminum foil!" he exclaimed and held up a well-preserved roll. "We can make hats out of this to keep our brains from frying."

"Yeah, man, that's good stuff. Hang on to it. We can use that for lots of things," said Joe as he uncovered a rusty knife, a spoon, and a syrup bottle. He kept them all, except the knife which he gave to Crowbar. He had one.

By nightfall they had trapped six more fish under stones, had dug up a peck of starchy cattail tubers, which they put in the partially empty grapefruit bag together with a mess of watercress. Just before dark they lit a small fire, cooked the carp, and ate the fruit of prickly-pear cactus raw. Crowbar made them each an aluminum foil hat. Joe suggested they wear their life jackets as long as it was practical for whatever use they might make of them, then stretched out in the cool grass. They listened to the plaintive voice of the phoebe announcing the end of the day and fell into a deep sleep.

In the predawn Joe awoke Crowbar, and after eating candy bars for breakfast, they shouldered water, food and rope, and started off. At the end of the canyon the way up was on crumbly shale that broke and slipped. Then, as if to make this ascent even more difficult, three ravens flew in off the river and, alighting inches ahead of them, focused their beady eyes on the food bag. Joe yelled at them; they floated up ahead and alighted again.

"I don't like those birds," said Crowbar as one turned over a pebble near his hand, pretending not to be interested in the bag of food. "They're scavengers. They're going to get our food one way or another. They're smart." He swatted at the raven and it brushed his eyes with its wings as it flew a few feet and set down again. Crowbar swore at it.

Joe took a long step, the shale slipped, and he went backward several feet before he could claw to a stop. Adjusting the bottles and the grapefruit bag, he dug in his toes again and, taking smaller steps, climbed back to where he had been. Crowbar, the heavy rope over his shoulder, worked his way upward, seemingly taking to shale climbing quite naturally; then the slope steepened and he could not make any headway. He sidestepped to an incline made of large chunks of shale and crawled upwards.

Joe, walking very carefully now, heard an explosion of rocks that announced Crowbar had taken a long slide. He looked down and saw his friend bent like a stretching yogi as he tried to stop himself from sliding. Finally he slowed down and came to a halt.

"What are you going down for?" teased Joe when he saw Crowbar was all right. Then a rock broke off in his hand and he slid twenty feet before coming to rest near Crowbar.

"I came down here to catch *you*," said Crowbar sarcastically.

44

They started up again, this time being very careful where they put their hands and feet.

The hours went by slowly. The sun climbed the sky and beat down on their heads like a hammer. Hot, dry winds sawed at their skin. Sipping water when their mouths became too dry to tolerate, wishing the treacherous climb on the loose shale would end, they crept up the great slope.

At noon they finally came off the shale onto firm sandstone and threw themselves down to rest. Joe passed one of the mayonnaise jars to Crowbar and he drank gratefully; then he noticed that a wall of quartzite sparked above their heads. It was almost two stories high.

"We can't climb that!" Crowbar exclaimed. "That's a sheet of glass." Joe agreed they should look for an easier route. He untied one of the bacon bars from his T-shirt, where he had knotted them, and passed half to Crowbar. As they ate and drank they leaned back against the blazing hot cliff and stared out upon the red, blue, green, and orange rocks that banded the entire landscape.

"At least the view is nice," said Crowbar, wiping the perspiration from his neck and arms.

"Yes, and we're making progress," said Joe, rising to go on. "The river's no longer in sight."

All afternoon they walked on the ledge of sandstone searching for a crack in the quartzite that they could climb. The wall was endless and before sundown they decided to stop and rest overnight.

"I'd thought we'd be on the Tonto Platform by now," said Crowbar, as he threw down his burden of rope. Joe said nothing, just picked up a stone and scratched a flat site on which to sleep. He picked dry grass, gathered a few woody centers of dead barrel cacti, and struck up a fire.

Crowbar wandered off, and Joe, taking his aluminum foil hat, wrapped a few of their fish and several frogs in it and placed them in the embers. He dusted off two flat stones for plates and put small piles of watercress on each. The table was set when Crowbar returned with fruits of the agave, one of the century plants.

"If they were good enough for my ancestors, they're good enough for me," he said and bit into what was once the staple food of the Havasupai Indians who had lived in the canyon for thousands of years. The fruit was not quite ripe and Crowbar's mouth puckered.

"Excellent," he lied and handed one to Joe, who, having noted Crowbar's face, put his in the foil with the fish.

"I'm going to cook mine," he said.

The juicy-sweet frogs' legs, the fruit, and long gulps of water put Joe and Crowbar in a victorious frame of mind. They sang by the campfire, accompanied by cicadas on the cacti, filing their wings together and amplifying the scratches a thousand-fold on tiny sound-increasing boxes at the base of their wings. Keeping beat with the throb of the insect chorus the boys invented a desert song.

"It's not far now," sang Crowbar, happier as the sun flashed suddenly and dropped behind the far rim.

The dawn was cool, around 80 degrees as opposed to 120 degrees during the day. Joe and Crowbar split a grapefruit, packed, and started along the wall in the hope, once more, of finding an easy route to the top of the quartzite.

The land was now bare and soulless. Tarantula wasps buzzed when they brushed against the pencil-like ocotillo plants, desert vegetation that could drop their leaves and live through long droughts. Collared lizards darted under the rocks as the boys approached. Then the living things no longer buzzed and scratched. The clatter of rolling stones from their feet became the only sound in the big void.

The sun brightened; the water in the jars and Clorox bottles went down and down.

Still there was no break in the hard white wall, and late in the afternoon Joe took stock of the water supply.

"We're going to have to climb this durn cliff." He looked up. "It's not so high here, less than fifty feet, I'd say. If we get to the top of the quartzite, there's a slope of mauve limestone. That'll be easy, and then we are faced with the Red Wall, five hundred feet of it. For that we're going to need every drop of water we have; but hopefully once on top of the Red Wall there'll be pockets of rainwater and an easy trail down into Havasu Canyon and the village."

"Let's go," said Crowbar, girding himself for the work ahead. He licked his cracked lips and studied the quartzite. Presently he coiled the rope neatly on the ground, took an end, twirled it over his head, and let go. It snaked up into the air and dropped over a stone outcrop. Crowbar fed out the length by whipping it, and presently the end of the rope came down to where they stood. He tied it to a rock and held the other end taut. Joe grabbed the rope and, feet on the wall, climbed hand over hand to the stone outcrop. Crowbar tied the food and water on the free end; Joe hauled them up. He then wrapped the rope around a rock so Crowbar could climb up. He did. Crowbar saw another outcrop higher, tossed the rope, and began the routine again.

At twilight they crept over the last of the quartzite and flopped onto the slope of mauve limestone. Crowbar untied the last gallon jar of water and gulped.

"Take it easy," said Joe. "That's all we've got except for what's in the wine bottle." He pointed to the distant flat top of the Red Wall where rain pockets might be. "And maybe it hasn't rained up there for days."

Crowbar took another long swallow. "We're okay. It can't be far." He reached for the food bag, and as he did so his arm hit the gallon jar. It toppled and smashed. The water sank into the ground and vanished.

Joe was horrified. The blazing desert with a wine bottle of water!

Crowbar rolled onto his side and covered his head. Joe felt sorry for him.

"Man," he said, "that's more like something I'd do, not you. If it hadn't been you, it would sure have been me." Crowbar did not answer.

Joe wedged the bottle safely in a crack in a rock and curled up in a ball. The sun went down, the blazing stars came out, and both boys lay wide-awake. Joe watched a dark rain cloud over the Colorado. Crowbar studied the Red Wall.

Many hours later Joe awoke to a slurping sound and rolled to his knees. Crowbar was sleeping soundly. He stood up and in the dim light of dawn saw the Lizard Boy squatting beside the grapefruit bag, eating the last fruit: rind, seeds, and pulp.

"Stop!" Joe yelled. The boy did not look up.

"I know you can hear. Gimme that!" He leaped toward the fruit, but the boy hopped out of reach with the ease of a raven.

Crowbar awoke. He saw the last grapefruit going into the Lizard Boy's gullet, rolled over on his stomach and moaned.

"We're dead," he said. "We're dead."

# The Lizard Boy

For a long, thoughtful moment, Joe stared at the boy squatting on the slope, the purple walls and pink spaces of the Grand Canyon hanging behind him.

This boy, he knew, was their salvation.

"Water," he said to him, pointing to the wine bottle. "Where can we get water?" The boy shook like a bird arranging its feathers and settled deeper into his trance.

"Water," Joe repeated. "Where's the water?" The boy continued to stare with nonseeing eyes. A dribble of grapefruit ran down his chin. He licked.

"The kid's incredible," said Crowbar. "He's really out to lunch. He doesn't even know we're here."

"Once there was a kid like this in France," said Joe. "He was called the Wild Boy of Aveyron. He lived alone in the woods on roots, fruits, and nuts. My brother Sam read all about him; said he never associated with people so he didn't need to talk. And like a hermit he lost the ability to hear or even see people." Joe went on, staring at the boy. "But our wild boy sure can hear, see, and smell what he needs, which is food. That we know."

"Did anyone ever teach that boy in France to talk?"

"A little."

"How?"

"I don't know. I didn't read the book."

"That figures."

"Lizard Boy likes chocolate bars," Joe went on, ignoring Crowbar. "We could hold one out and not give it to him until he said *chocolate*, like training a dog."

"The candy's all gone," said Crowbar.

"Well, maybe we can bribe him with other food."

Joe mentally counted their larder: fish, two bacon bars, some cattail tubers, and several green fruits of agave. Breaking a small piece off a bacon bar he held it out. The boy sniffed, then grabbed. Joe slopped the water in the wine bottle.

"Water." He pointed to the bottle. "Where can we get water?" The Lizard Boy looked down, scratched the soil and picked up a tiny seed. He popped it into his mouth.

"Forget teaching *him*," said Crowbar. "We'll dry up trying. We'd better get climbing."

The boy put his knuckles on the ground and inched closer to Joe. Despite his disappointment, Joe patted his mud-splattered shoulder.

"It's okay," he said. "It's not your fault. We got ourselves into this mess."

Slowly the boy turned his head and his eyes came into focus on Joe's hand. He squinted at it on his shoulders, and a small light of awareness gleamed in his deepset eyes. Joe took his hand away.

The boy stroked the spot where it had been. Joe patted him again.

"This kid's never been hugged, I bet," said Joe. His thoughts raced back to his father and the contentment he had felt when he was curled on his lap, strong arms around him.

"Do you remember how you learned to speak, Crowbar?" he asked. Crowbar shook his head.

Joe thought a moment, then took the Lizard Boy in his arms, stroked his hair, and pushed it out of his eyes. He hugged him close. The leathery little face almost smiled.

"Water," Joe said, bending down and scooping up imaginary water in his hands. "Water, water." The eyes filmed over and the boy's attention was gone.

"He doesn't get it," said Crowbar.

"Man, he's got to, or we'll fry." Joe hugged the child closer, rocking gently.

"Show him what water is," suggested Crowbar. "Not just what you do with it."

Joe poured a few drops of the precious water in his palm and held it under the boy's nose. He sniffed. Joe repeated the word. The face went blank. Joe dripped a few drops on his knee. The Lizard Boy licked it and laughed a strange laugh, more like the bray of a burro than the voice of a human child.

"Wow," said Joe. "This is a tough assignment."

Suddenly the boy's eyes shot to Joe's lips and he touched them. Something had clicked in the little fellow's head. A word, a sound, a phrase? What had he said? What? In desperation Joe tried: "Wow."

"Wow," the boy repeated slowly.

"WOW!" exclaimed Joe. "He spoke! He spoke!"

Afraid it was only an accident, he repeated the

sound. "Wow," the Lizard Boy answered more clearly.

"Now what do we do, Crowbar? We've got a sound, but it's got no meaning. How do we give it meaning?"

Rocking the child in his arms he touched the bottle to the boy's lips and moistened them with the water.

"Wow-ter," he said.

"Wow-ter," the boy repeated.

"Hey," gasped Crowbar. "He got it. Man, reward him. Reward him. Give hime something to eat." He searched his pocket and found a gummy piece of candy. "Gold star, like at school." At the rattle of the paper, the boy was upon the sweet. He stuffed it in his mouth and clawed at Crowbar's pants for more.

"Wow-ter," the boy said and his eyes shone with understanding. "Wow-ter." He poked his fingers into the pocket.

"Nuts," said Joe. "He's got it wrong. He thinks candy is water." Joe put his chin in his fists and pondered.

"Let's get out of here," said Crowbar. "This isn't going to work. And we'll die teaching him." He coiled the rope and shouldered it.

"We're not going far in this heat," said Joe. "Sit down. If we do anything, we should make a stone shelter and get in out of the sun till dusk. Shade drops the temperature ten degrees. We've only got a bottle of water. Remember?"

Crowbar's skin stretched and cracked as he moved in the heat. He dropped the rope, leaned down and picked up a stone slab. He began to build a shelter for the day.

The Lizard Boy watched the structure grow without much interest, but when it was done he crawled in and curled up. Joe and Crowbar joined him. They tried to sing, but the great hot silence swallowed their voices and enthusiasm. The boy leaned against Joe and he put his arm around him. He was not going to give up. The boy could say *wowter*. Now he must teach him what it meant.

As he dozed in the hot silence, Joe recalled learning the word *dog*. His father had pointed to a dog and said the word for it.

"Okay," he thought, discouraged by the slowness of his mind to see what must be done. "Lizard Boy knows what water is. He paddles in it. And he has a sound. How do I make them the same?"

The boy's eyes were open, gazing into space like a cat in a window. Joe patted his head and once more reached for the water bottle. He poured a drop on Lizard Boy's hand.

"Wow-ter." he said. The boy jumped to his feet and dashed out of the shelter. He came back with a lizard.

"Wow-ter, wow-ter," he spluttered, then jumped on Crowbar and pulled at his pocket. "Wow-ter."

"No!" screamed Joe in exasperation. He grabbed the Lizard Boy's shoulders and shook him so hard his mouth blubbered. "Don't you understand? Water, water." Clutching the bottle, he threw half of it on the boy's face. "Water! We need it!" The Lizard Boy covered his head with his arms, rolled into a ball, and wailed.

"Oh, nuts," Joe said. "I've hurt his feelings. That was a dumb thing to do. You can't get mad at a kid who can't understand you. I give up." Joe pushed back in the shelter. The boy lifted his head, saw that Joe was not going to shake him again, got up and ran off.

Crowbar, lying awake, remained silent. For a long time they stared out at the blue-shadowless canyon.

"We could go back to the river," Crowbar finally said.

"I don't know where it is," Joe admitted. "I got mixed up following that quartzite band." He took a deep breath: "So I've *got* to teach that kid to speak."

The sun climbed to the top of the sky, its brilliance filling the canyon with such intense light that barely a rim or a wall was visible. The huge canyon seemed to be all light and space.

Half-sleeping, half-thinking, Joe saw the Lizard Boy come back. He squatted by the door in the sun, apparently immune to the terrible heat rays. An hour passed, another and another. The sound of the breathing of all three rose and fell.

"Maybe I should draw a river in the dust," said Joe suddenly to no one in particular. "Got to talk to that kid."

"Let's get out of here," said Crowbar, getting to his feet. "We're drying up while we wait. We only have to go a quarter of a mile straight up. Then we'll be on the Tonto Platform."

"We can't walk a step in this heat without water," snapped Joe, and he pulled Crowbar back into the shade. "At least wait for twilight. We'll use up less fluids if we walk in the cool."

Crowbar flopped back into the shelter, grumbling. Joe yelled at him. He yelled back and the Lizard Boy whined and got up. Leaping like a goat he disappeared around the curve of the mesa.

"Gone," said Joe. "That's that."

They dozed, awakened, passed the bottle back and forth to moisten their mouths, and finally slept.

Hours later, when twilight cooled the air, Joe rolled to his elbows. He thought he smelled water. He saw that Lizard Boy was back and curled close to him, staring into his eyes.

"Wow-ter," said the boy with a frightened look.

"Yeah, wow-ter," snapped Joe. "Where the devil is it?"

The boy nuzzled his head against Joe. Joe sat bolt upright. The boy's hair was wet. Incredulously he stroked the matted hair.

"Water! My God, Crowbar! Wake up. His hair's wet. He's found water." Joe hugged the boy, then took him in his arms and rocked him.

"Good boy!" he exclaimed. "Good boy!"

The Lizard Boy broke away and getting to his feet jumped up and down in excitement.

"Wow-ter, wow-ter," he repeated, imitating Joe's own laugh.

"Where is it?" Joe almost cried as a landslide of problems occurred to him. "He knows water, but how do we teach him *Take us to the water?*"

"With verbs and prepositions and pronouns," Crowbar answered sarcastically.

"Thanks."

Suddenly the Lizard Boy picked up the wine bottle and dumped out the last drops. He threw down the vessel and ran.

"Come back," yelled Joe.

"I'm going to beat his tail," said Crowbar, picking up the rope.

Joe grabbed the string with the food bag and empty jar, and chased after Crowbar and the kid.

They rounded buttes, slipped on shaly slopes,

scrambled up a rock pile and, yelling, shouting, keeping an eye on the Lizard Boy, came around a mesa and found him with his back against a wall. He sidestepped to a crack and disappeared.

"This is insane," Joe said and sat down. "We're sweating and using up all our body fluids." Pulling a new aluminum foil hat over his eyes, his life jacket over his head, he stared at his sneakers.

"The platform's only a quarter of a mile up," said Crowbar.

"A quarter of a mile is a million," Joe snorted.

A lizard darted between his feet; he pounced on it, took a bite, and spit it out. "Ugh!" He threw it down. Crowbar snatched it up.

"You can't be so choosy," he said, popped it into his mouth, gagged, but swallowed it.

"There's a touch of water in it." He wiped his mouth and looked for another.

The hot sun was now gone, but its fire was still in the rocks and they sent up burning heat waves.

"I'm too thirsty to think," said Joe, and he stretched out to wait for darkness. Perhaps the dew would fall before he died.

"You turn black when you die of thirst," said Crowbar.

"Nifty," answered Joe, and he stared at the cloudless sky.

A sliced moon came up.

"We've been gone a long time," Joe observed as he measured the wane of the moon. Licking his cracked and bleeding lips he got to his feet. His tongue was a ball of cotton in his mouth.

Painfully he and Crowbar crept along the escarpment, moving slowly toward the ledge where the Lizard Boy had vanished.

A spidery shadow darted along the wall above

them; then the boy dropped down beside Joe and held out his arms to be hugged. He was dripping wet.

"Wow-ter," he said.

Joe drew him close and patted him on the head. "You bet, wow-ter," he said. "Where is it?"

The boy only nuzzled Joe for more hugs.

Crowbar knotted, then slipped the rope around Lizard Boy's waist.

"I'm hanging on to this kid until he gets us to that water," he said.

The rope tightened, the boy's eyes flashed with terror and he clawed Crowbar, then ran straight up the wall. Yelling at him to stop, Crowbar climbed after him.

"Don't hurt him," Joe shouted and clambered after them both.

"Hey," called Crowbar, "there's a break in the wall. We can climb to the platform here. It's easy." He gave the boy a tug.

"Wow-ter," the Lizard Boy said and pulled the other way.

"This way!" Crowbar forcibly yanked the boy.

"Follow him, you nut," Joe shouted in anger. "He's trying to take us to water."

"Yeah? To a batch of candy bars or lizards?" Yet he did not insist. He turned around and the three climbed down a slab, rounded a butte, and came upon a cave. It was high on the wall, one like those the ancient Indian cave dwellers might have lived in.

The Lizard Boy got down on hands and knees and they followed him under an arch and out into a water-carved canyon. Joe smelled the dampness, then heard the bubbling, cool sound. A stream splashed down the rocks in moonlight and lay in silver pools among whispering trees.

Joe hugged the child. Crowbar cheered, threw down the rope, and fell face first into the pool.

While the Lizard Boy squatted on the shore, Joe and Crowbar absorbed the water through pores, mouths, and eyes. They splashed, laughed, and lay back in the clear water. Finally Joe came ashore and sat down beside the boy.

"Wowter," The boy said and sidled close to him, visibly excited by the connection between the sound he had made and the water.

"Yes, wowter," said Joe, and splashed him. "Water." He patted it on his cheeks and hugged him once again.

"Wow-ter." The child's husky voice trembled with the thrill of his success.

# Inner Kingdom

Joe slept fitfully. The Lizard Boy was tied to a tree. Last night Crowbar had decided to keep him leashed until they could teach him *Take us to the village.* Joe had agreed; but the boy's high-pitched whine had disturbed his sleep all night, and now that the dawn was coming he could stand it no longer. He arose and went to the Lizard Boy.

Reaching into his pocket Joe took out a piece of bacon bar and put it under the boy's nose. He sniffed, grabbed it, and stuffed it into his mouth. While he was chewing, Joe dug a long trench in the clay and carefully placed several small square stones to represent houses; he poked leafy plants beside the houses for trees.

"Village," he said. "Supai village. Do you know where it is? We must get there."

The Lizard Boy swallowed the piece of bacon bar and, leaping to his feet, shot his hand into the bushes. When he pulled it out he had four bird's eggs which he promptly ate. Joe waited until he had his attention again.

"Supai village."

The boy whined, then he picked up the rope and attempted to chew it in half. Joe could not bear the sight any longer. He untied the boy.

Instantly he broke into a run, splashed through a pool, and sprinted up a staircase of cascades to the far end of the canyon. Moving like a swallow, he darted up the wall and disappeared into a crevasse as if he had been there many times.

Joe thought about that. This land was familiar to the Lizard Boy. He *must* know where the Indian village was; he not only traveled far in the Grand Canyon, but he seemed quite at home wherever they came upon him, up the side canyons as well as on the river.

Joe did not go after the boy. He had learned *water*; he could learn *village*, but it was going to take time. Joe scanned their canyon, taking stock of the food resources.

The canyon was shaped like a horseshoe with smooth orange walls about seventy feet high. A green carpet of plants flourished along a stream that was a staircase of cascades and pools. The pool dams were curved, for they were made of travertine, a stone that precipitates out of the limy canyon water and forms circular walls. The many tadpoles in the pool told Joe there was a good supply of frogs, and through the clear water he saw fish. Small birds were numerous, and mice and lizards darted over and under rocks. Around the stream, enormous cottonwoods and velvet ash trees shaded the grasses and flowers.

Joe walked to the spring that was the source of the

stream. An abundance of watercress and monkey flowers grew around it, both nourishing plants, Joe recalled having read. Maidenhair fern was bountiful in the spray zone of the cascades and he tasted a leaf to see if it was edible. He concluded that it would pass if it were boiled with garlic. As he walked back to Crowbar he gathered some wool from the Rocky Mountain sheep that had pulled off on many of the twigs, and thought about uses for it — pillows, string, chinking cracks.

Near the largest pool he caught two frogs. But his best find was behind a rock, where he came upon a patch of Indian vine, a wild plant that produces squash. One was ripe; he picked it and hurried back to Crowbar, who was still asleep under the cottonwood tree.

"Wake up!" he yelled. "It's time for school. We have to start by being teachers."

Crowbar sat straight up, moaned, and shook his head. Slowly he opened his eyes.

"Hey, where am I?" He rubbed his eyes. "Have I died and gone to heaven? This place is beautiful."

"I am glad you like it," Joe said. "You may be here a long time. Lizard Boy no talkee *village*."

Crowbar barely heard, he was so charmed by the green trees, red and gold flowers, birds, and the blue tumbling water.

"This is a whole kingdom," he said. "It's got birds and beasts and fruits and . . ." — he picked up a squarish stone — "it's even got building blocks. We'll build ourselves a castle."

"There seems to be enough food for the time being," Joe said, looking around at the natural resources. Crowbar went on with his own theme.

"And we'll dub this place the Inner Kingdom. The

Havasupais call the world beyond the Grand Canyon the Outer Kingdom, so this has got to be the Inner Kingdom."

"Inner Kingdom? Build a castle! Crowbar, are you out of your mind? What about your mother? Don't you think she'll have the whole United States Army out looking for us?"

"Joe, they're going to find the shreds of that raft and think we're dead."

"Not Uncle Como," said Joe firmly. "But I guess he'll tell the authorities just as a last resort, so as not to get us thrown in jail. We'd better concentrate on getting ourselves out."

"Speaking of which," said Crowbar picking up the untied rope, "we've just lost our lifeline. Lizard Boy is gone."

A rock fell off the wall, bounced to the bottom and rolled against the cottonwood tree where they stood. Joe looked up. The boy was squatting on his heels, staring at them without seeing.

"He's loose!" exclaimed Crowbar.

"I let him go. We can't tie him up. . . . We really can't."

"Yeah," said Crowbar thoughtfully. "He speaks. He's a person. He can't be owned." Their eyes met and for a moment each wondered what the other was thinking.

When Crowbar had a fire going, Joe gutted and skinned the two frogs and thought about how to teach the Lizard Boy the word *village*. Intent upon his thoughts and work, he did not see the boy approach, sniffing as he came, until he pounced for the frogs. But not quickly enough. Joe snatched them up first. With a scowl he wrapped them in foil and placed them on the fire.

63

"He's got the nose of a hound dog," said Crowbar, who had been watching the performance. "Do you suppose that's how he finds the lizards and birds?"

As if in answer the boy stood up, sniffed the air, and darted into a bed of ferns. He came back with a snake, killed it, and walked to the fire. He shoved it in the flames.

"Cook," said Joe. "You are cooking."

The boy did not seem to hear. He squatted, watching the flames with unusual concentration. A moment passed. Presently he reached into the hot coals and, grabbing his snake as well as the frogs, ran off eating.

"No!" Crowbar roared. "Man, we've got to teach him *no* before we teach him *village*."

"There's so much we've got to teach him," said Joe. "I never knew how complicated words are until now."

Crowbar tested the plumpness of the Indian squash Joe had brought back, wrapped it in tinfoil and pushed it into the coals.

"Anyone for squash?" he said, and laughed halfheartedly.

While it cooked they gathered a good supply of firewood, then filled the grapefruit bag with starchy cattail roots. Returning to the campsite they found the Lizard Boy squatting beside the fire. He grunted and poked a finger toward the hot coals.

"Cook," he said.

"Hey, that's great," exclaimed Joe. Before he could hug him in approval, the boy slipped into the pool without causing a ripple. In a moment he surfaced with a trout in his teeth and brought it flopping to the fire.

"Cook," he repeated with more confidence, and thrust the fish toward the flames. Truly excited by the Lizard Boy's progress, Joe cleaned the fish, wrapped it in the remaining foil, and shoved it in the fire.

"Cook." Joe demonstrated, then he slipped his arm around the boy and gave him a squeeze.

The child's patience was short, however, and in less than a minute he had pulled the fish out of the fire and gobbled part of it virtually raw. His hunger was satisfied for the moment and he dropped the rest of the fish on the ground. Crowbar gingerly picked it up and replaced it on the coals.

In a squatting position the child hopped sideways to him.

"Village," Crowbar said and pointed to Joe, himself, and the boy, but his voice was not heard by the Lizard Boy. He was asleep on his haunches in accordance with his own rhythm of food and rest.

"It's going to take a long time to teach this kid," Joe said. "Let's get going on Inner Kingdom."

Crowbar nodded and walked to the edge of the stream. "First, we need a shelter from the sun and rain. I'll build a structure over here." He gestured toward the wall that rose out of the meadow.

"Then we're going to need hooks and lines to catch fish," said Joe, taking the squash out of the coals and sharing it with Crowbar.

"I think a net would be more efficient. I can make one out of cattail leaves," replied Crowbar.

"We've got plenty of lizards," said Joe, tallying his morning inventory. "A few agave, lots of prickly-pears, watercress, squash, tadpoles, and if we can figure out how to make a trap, we could get a mountain sheep." Joe leaned down and picked up the shell of the squash they had eaten. "And here's a bowl," he said, holding it up.

"And here comes tonight's dinner," said Crowbar as two ravens dropped into the canyon and perched on a limb above their heads, eyes on the guts of the fish and frogs at the pool's edge.

"Ah ha!" exclaimed Crowbar, seeing their intent. Quickly he unwound a strand from the rope, looped it into a slipknot, and encircled the fish guts. Holding the end of the line, he wiggled out of sight under a patch of monkey flowers.

"Walk away," he said to Joe. "Birds can't count."

The Lizard Boy was still asleep by the fire, and Crowbar let him remain there. He looked like a rock, even to a raven.

As Joe walked away, one of the ravens dropped down from the tree and landed on the entrails. Crowbar yanked and caught the bird's foot in the snare.

"BROOOOOOOOOOOCK!" The raven's scream was a bloodcurdling alarm that brought the Lizard Boy to his feet and Joe splashing down the stream bed.

Crowbar fell on the raven; Joe jumped over the monkey flowers, but his help was not needed. The bird went into shock, rolled its eyes, fell on its back and lay still. As Crowbar triumphantly removed the string from its leg, it instantly revived and bit his hand so hard he yelled and let go. The raven was free.

It beat one full wing stroke and no more. The Lizard Boy leaped, caught the bird in the air, and doubled over it. When he straightened up, raven feathers clung to his mouth; the bird was dead.

"Cook," he said, and squatted by the dying fire.

"He's got *that* all right," said Crowbar. "He'll even catch a bird on the wing for some home cooking." Crowbar wiped his forehead, astounded by what he had just beheld. "This kid is smart, Joe. Let's get on with his lessons." He turned to the

Lizard Boy. "Take us to the village, the village, people, houses."

The boy's eyes dimmed as he hunched over the dead bird.

"You're going too fast," said Joe. "I'm slow-witted, so I know how long it takes to learn something. First of all, what is a village? A lot of people living near each other. He can't know what a village is until he knows what people are."

"You're right. Well, how do we teach him *people*?"

The child straightened up and, placing the bird in the embers, hopped toward Joe.

"Wow-ter," he said.

"Nuts, we're losing ground." Joe snapped his fingers in discouragement. "He's forgotten what water means."

"Maybe he wants to parboil the bird," said Crowbar, now impatient again with the whole idea of schooling the boy. He strode off to the area he had designated for a shelter and started clearing away the weeds and brush.

Gently Joe took the boy's hand, asking himself how the child could know what people were until he knew what he was. Thoughtfully he led the Lizard Boy to a still pool above the camp and, putting his arm around him, pointed to their reflections in the water. The boy looked at Joe, then followed his gaze to the water.

Joe stuck out his tongue at himself and wagged his fingers on his ears. The boy looked at him. Having his attention, Joe pointed to his image. The child glanced at the water, then at Joe, and finally at the water. Suddenly he smiled, reached down to the bottom of the pool, picked up a snail, and ate it.

"Oh, nuts," Joe snorted, realizing the boy had

seen right through the water. "This isn't going to work."

Joe lay down on his stomach above the pool and the Lizard Boy rocked off his knees and onto his stomach. Together they peered into the water. Joe pointed to their reflections again, then reached over and patted the Lizard Boy's cheek. This time the boy saw something, for he turned his head and stared at Joe, then looked back into the water. The child's eyes shifted from Joe to Joe's reflection.

"Ow, ow, ow," he wailed, and grabbed Joe as if to save him from the water.

"That's me," he said, not understanding the boy's problem. And so the child kept screaming.

"Lost cause," he said and rocked back to his heels, cutting off his reflection. "Scratch this plan. He can't see himself. "I've got to go back to the beginning."

He hugged his knees. "He knows *water* and *cook*. Now, what follows next?" He thought a minute. "Lizards; he knows what lizards are, so I'll teach him that next. First I'll review *water* and *cook* and graduate to *lizard*, and then, object by object, work up to *village*."

"Water," Joe said, splashing the surface.

"Wow-ter," the boy said, and when the ripples died, he pointed to Joe's reflection. "Wow-ter."

"No . . . well, yes," Joe said, realizing suddenly that the boy did not know his name so had used the sound that he knew best.

"Joe," he pronounced clearly and pointed to his reflection. The boy stared at the image then turned and looked at him. Joe pointed to himself. "Joe."

"Choe," said the child, slowly rising to his knees to touch his face. "Choe," he whispered.

"Right." Joe kept his voice calm. "Choe. I'm Choe. You are . . ." Suddenly he realized he had no name for the child. He could not call him Lizard Boy; that was demeaning. He must be given a name, one with dignity. *Wow* had been his first sound and *water* his first word. He would name him *Walter*.

Taking the boy's shoulders in his hands, Joe once more squared him around until they were face to face. The boy's eyes focused on the ground, then on Joe's hands, and finally on his eyes. At last Joe had his full attention.

"Choe," he said, pointing to himself. Then he pointed to the Lizard Boy and turned him so that he was looking down at his own reflection.

"Walter. You are Walter."

The gnarled brown fingers tightened on the rock as Walter stared long at his own reflection. Then he sat up and peered into Joe's face. His brows knitted together, his nostrils flared in and out, and the alertness that came across the boy's face when he saw food now lit his features again.

"Walter," he said, pointing to himself. His calloused hand touched Joe's face like a butterfly wing.

"Choe," he said.

"Man, that's right! That's it!" Joe threw his arms around him, then reached into his pocket for the last bit of bacon bar. Walter glanced at it and, pushing it away, lay on his stomach and stared down into the pool. He shoved the hair off his face and touched his nose. For a long time he studied his own reflection, pulling an ear and sticking out his tongue. Joe had never seen him concentrate so intensely before and he felt for the first time that victory was not far away.

The sun climbed the sky, the birds quieted down for their midday siesta, and the boy still gazed upon his own reflection. Finally a frog leaped into the pool and ripples fractured Walter's image into rings of many dark faces. Joe waited to see if the sight of so many Walters would be frightening, but when the boy got to his feet the corners of his lips were curled. Of course, Joe thought, he has seen frog and fish circles a thousand times. Ripples are not new to him.

As Walter stood on the rock in the sun the elation on his face died and he ran past Joe without seeing him. Climbing to his crevasse on the wall, he squatted, bowed his head, and went to sleep. He relieved himself as he dozed.

Joe had lost him again, but by now he knew it was only a matter of time before Walter would ask for more lessons. He wanted to learn.

Joe went back to their campsite and picked up the grapefruit bag. He had an idea to simplify fishing and tadpole catching. He could use the bag as a net. Scrambling back to the spring he dragged it through the water where the tadpoles lay. With a quick yank he pulled up and caught three.

"Ha," he shouted and looked up to see Walter watching him. The boy's eyes misted over and he dropped his head back onto his knees.

On the way home he found another squash that was ripe, then walked briskly to the far end of the canyon, to see if he could execute an idea he had to make a bighorn sheep trap. He had noticed hoofprints around the spring this morning and envisioned digging a hole and covering it with brush so that when the sheep came down to drink they would fall in.

Selecting a sheep trail through the bushes, he began digging with a flat, sharp stone. The soil was gravelly and hard, and after almost five hours of work, his hunger drove him back to camp. As he passed the crevasse where Walter slept, he paused.

"Walter," he called. Instantly the boy stood up, swung down the rocks, and followed him through the tall grass and wildflowers back to their campsite under the cottonwood trees.

Crowbar was hauling a large squarish rock across the meadow to the canyon wall. He dropped it and came running back.

"You got Lizard Boy," he cried. "Good, I get nervous when he runs out of sight."

"Don't call him Lizard Boy anymore. He's got a name now. It's Walter. Watch this." Joe took Walter's hand and placed it against his own chest.

"Choe," the boy said. Then Joe put his hand on him.

"Walter," he answered, his eyes shining with pleasure. Crowbar's mouth dropped open in amazement. Joe grinned with pride and put his hand on Crowbar. Turning to Walter, he hesitated.

"Tarzan," he said.

"Tarzan," repeated Walter clearly. "Tarzan."

Joe grinned, Crowbar snarled, chuckled, then burst into laughter. Walter's eyes were bright with excitement, and again Joe took the opportunity to teach. Pointing to himself, Crowbar, and Walter, he made an all-encompassing gesture.

"People," he said. The boy's face dulled, his eyes widened. and he curled up his lips.

"No! No!" he blurted, and jumped up and down in frustration.

"Walter, Choe, Tarzan." He put his arms around them. "Walter, Choe, Tarzan."

"PEOPLE," snapped Crowbar. "We are all people, Walter! Choe, you, and Tarzan, PEOPLE." Crowbar's voice approached a scream and Walter pulled away. The voice frightened him, perhaps because angry sounds were associated with the huge welts on his body. Walter ran. Joe spun around and faced Crowbar.

"Lay off," he said in anger. "He *is* learning. But it's slow. We got to keep taking one thing at a time."

"He's an idiot, and he doesn't know where the village is." Crowbar gave Joe a shove. "Come here and see what I've done. At least we'll stay alive until someone finds us."

He led Joe to the canyon edge where he had stacked flat sandstones one upon another against the wall to make a large lean-to. Limbs placed across the top were thatched over with the long leaves of the cattails. Cool shadows fell in the room, and moss gathered by Crowbar carpeted the floor.

He pointed to two piles of leaves and said they were beds. "Yours and mine." Then he added: "This is our home, 20 Canyon Street, Inner Kingdom, U.S.A."

"Gee, it's swell," said Joe, peering admiringly at the neatly built walls and soft beds.

"That's not all." He led Joe to their fireplace beside the stream. "Here's the kitchen." He gestured to a large thin slab of stone balanced on a smaller squarish boulder.

"Kitchen table," Crowbar said, patting it.

"How did you get this up there?" asked Joe as he touched the three-by-four-foot stone tabletop.

"Crowbars," he answered and winked. "And now for the stove." Joe turned around and saw that the open fire was now enclosed in three neatly stacked walls. A stony spit lay across the top like a grill. Joe turned it over and saw that it was one of the sticks that had fallen into the stream and become covered with travertine. It was now a stone pole. He stepped to the stream, picked up another, and realized they had a great natural resource in these stone logs. He turned the log over.

"I'm building a sheep pit," he said, "but this gives

me a better idea. I'll make a trap that the sheep wander into but can't get out of, like corrals on a cattle ranch."

"Yeah," said Crowbar, "that's a good idea but come here, you haven't seen all I've done."

He led Joe around a bulge in the canyon wall. Behind it lay a gravel bed where the rain washed away from 20 Canyon Street and the kitchen.

"The privy," he said. "That narrow flat stone against the wall is the shovel. The round stones in the wash are the toilet paper."

"I think we're going to have some trouble with Walter in this area," Joe said.

"So I've noticed."

As they walked back to the kitchen they passed 20 Canyon Street and Joe once more peered in. Walter was curled in the leaves and moss, his hands over his head, his eyes out of focus, a crooked smile on his face.

"I'll bet Walter's going to learn fast now," Joe said. "He's sleeping indoors, like us. If he keeps copying what we do he'll learn pretty fast."

The evening meal was short on meat, for Joe had only caught three tadpoles that morning and the raven took too long to cook. The baked cattails were filling but not a hit.

"Too tough," said Crowbar, chewing on one. "Something's got to be done about this. We need something to grind them into powder."

After dinner Joe plucked the raven to prepare it for the next day's menu. Then he tilted a stone to make a backrest, and watched the fire fade from embers to gray coals.

The stars came out, Crowbar stopped working, and they retired to 20 Canyon Street.

# 20 Canyon Street

A few days later Joe spread about a dozen long cattail leaves side by side on the ground near the kitchen table. Taking another he began weaving it in and out. The breeze rustled the cottonwoods, and a canyon wren sang its flute song. He hummed and worked contentedly. Walter crouched beside him, watching and carefully sniffing the project. Suddenly he ran off.

Crowbar meandered down from the stream bank where he had been digging a millstream. "What are you doing?" he asked.

"Making a seine for fish. The grapefruit bag's too small," said Joe.

Crowbar scratched his head and studied the cattail mat. "Looks pretty flimsy to me. What we need is some nylon or something we can knot into a mesh. The weaving is too loose."

"Well, I'll just run right down to the store and

get some," said Joe, weaving another strip under the first.

"Did you check the sheep trap?" asked Crowbar.

"Yep. I've got to make it wider. They came down to the spring to drink, but slipped around the outside. All I need is three more posts and we'll have roast lamb." He readied another cattail leaf for weaving and rocked back on his heels. "I found where the sheep enter the canyon. Down a wide trail that looks like it might have been man-made."

"Put that damn thing down and let's have a look. We've got Walter for a fishnet. We don't need anything better. By the way, where is he?" Crowbar was constantly worried that the boy might leave and never come back.

Joe glanced around and then pointed. "Coming down from the top of the canyon with an armload of yucca leaves."

"Yucca leaves?" Crowbar scratched his head as Walter loped to the table, threw down the leaves, and began pounding them with a rock. Juices sprayed out, the table became green and sticky, but Walter worked on. Presently he took the mass to the stream and after dunking it up and down, held up a large ball of fiber. He tied a stone to a few threads and, spinning the stone with his hand, worked his fingers up and down the fiber. A cord formed before their eyes.

Wondering what he was going to do next, Joe and Crowbar watched Walter pull the grapefruit bag out of the stream where it had been tied to keep the food cool. The boy studied the mesh and tried to speak, but he had no words for his thoughts.

"Hey," said Joe. "He's making a net. He saw me catch tadpoles with that bag. He's making a better fishnet!"

Pointing at the clumsy thing Joe had been trying to make, Walter shook his head and, twirling the stone, fed more threads into the forming string. Joe swung his leg over the stone chair, sat down, and began tying knots in the string. Crowbar grinned, picked up some hemp, a stone, and he spun thread too. By early evening they had about a square yard of netting.

"Net," said Joe.

"Net," answered Walter.

Joe put poles on each side of the mesh, then handed one to Crowbar. Together they splashed into the water and, pushing the net at an angle, one edge on the bottom, moved it upstream to a travertine dam. There they lifted it. Two nice trout flopped in the bottom.

"Terrific!" shouted Joe as he flung the fish onshore and waded out with Crowbar to seine the next pool.

Walter, who was watching from the shore, jumped up and down as his two friends splashed and shouted and caught another fish.

When they had enough for dinner they came back to the kitchen and prepared the fish for the grill Crowbar had made.

"He's not so dumb after all," said Crowbar. "I wonder where he learned about yucca string?"

"He's smart enough to figure it out for himself," snapped Joe.

After dinner Walter went off to 20 Canyon Street. Joe and Crowbar decided to check the sheep trap before retiring, and first Crowbar, then Joe dove into the deepest pool and, shouting joyfully, swam to the other side. Emerging wet they ran up the trail to the canyon head, flapping their shirts in the air to dry them.

"Laundry's done," quipped Joe. "Let's go to the

sheep trap first. We need food." Selecting several stone poles from the stream, he led Crowbar to the trap, a funnel of stakes that narrowed and opened into a large pen.

"Sheep are so dumb," he said, "they'll go into something like this, but can't figure how to get out." He showed Crowbar where the sheep had gotten around the mouth of the funnel, without entering it. Together they made it flush to the wall with stones and poles.

When they were satisfied that nothing could avoid the maze, Joe led Crowbar to a wide trail that began behind a clump of willows. It switched back and forth up the cliff, to almost the top.

"This *does* look man-made," said Crowbar as they walked up the trail around a pinnacle and out onto a wide flat shelf. Joe stepped to the right and saw a large squarish hole in which old beams were propped.

"A mine," he exclaimed. "A lot of mineral prospectors came down here in the early part of the century." He walked to the gaping cavern and, peering in, saw piles of small rocks and a few glittering pieces of quartz crystal.

"Looks like he was trying for gold," said Crowbar, picking up the tailings and running them through his fingers. Glittering bits of quartz fell sparkling into the sun, but no gold.

The stones above his head avalanched and Crowbar looked up.

"Hey!" Walter was standing above him. "I thought you were in bed."

"Choe, Tarzan," the boy said and walked along a ledge to another man-made hole they had not seen. He picked up a piece of pipe about six feet long.

"Hey, let me have that," exclaimed Crowbar. "I

can use that." Scrambling up the wall he flung his leg over the ledge and looked around.

"Man, there's some good stuff here," he called down to Joe. "Bolts, hunks of metal, a rusted saw, half a shovel, chain, wooden beams, a gear! Man this is just what I need. I'll make Inner Kingdom into Leisure City."

Crowbar handed the pipe down to Joe, put a bolt in his pocket and was about to pass down the gear when Walter picked up the chain, tied it to the gear, and lowered it to the bottom of the canyon. Crowbar blushed.

"And I thought he was dumb," he said, attaching some poles, the shovel, and saw to another length of chain.

The sun was almost down when they got back to the kitchen. Joe was ready to turn in for the day, but not Crowbar. He immediately began digging a small channel from an upper pool toward the low cliff at the upstream end of their meadow. He set the length of pipe into the ditch, let the water flow down it and splash in a stream to the ground below. Taking two of the beams, he pounded them close together near the falling water and went to the kitchen for the plastic Clorox bottle they had found at the river. With his sharpened knife he made a scoop of the bottle, and attached it to one end of a long pole he cut from a tree. He tied a huge rock to the other end, carved a hole in the middle of the pole, and suspended the pole between the beams. Pushing the bolt through the beams and pole, he tested it with his hand. Now he put a flat stone beneath the rock on the pole, and adjusted the pipe so that the water fell into the scoop. It filled, grew heavy, and dropped to the ground. The rock went up in the air. The scoop emptied. The rock fell down with a crash. The lightened scoop popped up, was filled with water from the pipe, and fell again.

Crowbar had made a plumping mill. He put a cattail tuber on the flat stone under the rock, and waited. Up went the rock, then down; the tuber was crushed to powder.

"We'll have no more tough roots," he said to himself, and stepping back to admire his work he tripped over Walter.

"Hey, what are you doing here?" Crowbar asked, but the boy did not hear him. He was watching the water flow down the pipe, fill the contraption, drop the rock, and crush the tuber.

The next morning he was back, staring at the plumping mill, watching in fascination.

After breakfast Crowbar went to get the gear and several short boards left at the foot of the canyon. Returning to the kitchen, he began digging again, this time with the rusty shovel, which enabled him to proceed rapidly.

Joe hunted cattails and squash. Several hours passed before he returned to the kitchen.

"Now what are you doing?" he said.

"No more hauling water, you'll see."

"But we don't have to haul it more than fifteen steps," Joe complained. "You'd better help me gather vegetables and catch fish. We've got to store up some food if we are going to walk out of here."

"What makes you think I'm going to?"

Joe stared at his friend, refusing to answer his baffling remark, then waded into the stream with the net. Crowbar jogged off to the foot of the canyon for more junk.

"JOE!" Crowbar's call was urgent. Splashing out of the water Joe threw down the net and bolted up the bank to his sheep trap. He rounded the spring and stopped.

There in the maze was a burro and her long-legged foal with huge oval eyes, blunt nose, and soft woolly body. "Geez, we can't eat them!" he exclaimed.

"Durn right we can," said Crowbar. "Burro is no tougher than sheep. Besides, we can tenderize it in the plumping mill." He turned around. "I'll get the rope. I know how to make a hangman's noose. We'll have food for months."

Joe leaned on the fence and stared at the two captives who swished flies with their tails and stared back.

"I don't know," he said, feeling his stomach churn at the thought of killing the burro. "Guess even after all this, I'm still a coward."

As Crowbar's footsteps died away the reeds rustled and Walter appeared. He glanced at the animals, then, face white with horror, jumped at Joe, snarling and spitting. Throwing back his head he brayed mournfully. The mother burro pricked her ears forward, sniffed the air, and brayed back. Walter leaped the fence and trotted around the corral, drumming a signal to the burros with the heels of his feet.

The mare stamped back and whinnied. Walter whinnied, then pawed the ground with his foot. The mare reared, eyes rolling with excitement. Joe gasped at the incredible performance, then Crowbar returned with the noose.

"They're talking to each other," Joe said incredulously. "Walter and the burros. That mare knows Walter. Look at her."

80

Walter rubbed his chin on her neck; she rubbed hers across his back. With that the foal jumped backward, pressing his ears back in terror. His mother whinnied, the foal relaxed and walked up to Walter. Sniffing, tossing his head, the young burro bucked and kicked. Walter bucked and kicked. He brayed, and throwing himself upon the mare's back let her carry him around in circles. The understanding that existed between child and beasts was clear, but what it all meant was mysterious.

"Geez, we've been trying to teach him English," Joe said. "All we need to do is say 'take me to the village' in donkeyese."

"I guess we don't eat burro," concluded Crowbar, dropping the noose. "Walter, methinks, would vanish forever if we harmed one hair on the beasties' heads." Joe nodded.

While they wondered what to do next, Walter slid off the mare, ran under her belly, and bumped her teats with his nose. She let down her milk and he sucked.

"Milk is excellent food," said Crowbar. With a single jerk he undid the noose and wound the rope back and forth across the entrance to the enclosure. Walter had calmed the mare and she him. All three seemed content in the corral.

That evening Joe placed beside each stone plate, knives and forks that he had whittled from a cottonwood limb. He made a paste of the cattail flour and baked big cakes on a hot stone; then, removing three large trout from the grill, garnished them with maidenhair ferns and whistled for his friends to come to dinner. Down the path came Crowbar, a gourd held high above his head. He was muddy and dirty, but the gourd was half full of rich, thick milk.

"She's a mean one," he said, and grinned. "Tossed me around a bit, but I milked her."

"Where's Walter?" Joe asked, looking toward 20 Canyon Street.

"He's up top. He ran off when I tried to milk the mare," Crowbar said. "But it's okay . . . he learned a new word . . . *grass* . . . and went off to find some. He probably knows just what they like."

"Well," grinned Joe. "We've got ourselves a dairy." He sipped the milk. "It's good," he said.

Halfway through the meal Walter slipped into his seat, and picking up his fork, turned it over and bit it in half before Joe could show him what to do with it.

"Nuts," Joe said. "Here I go pushing him again. I sort of hoped the knives and forks would recall a village to him, some town where he had lived in a house and eaten at a table. . . . It's been several days since I've tried to teach him *people* and *village*. I thought maybe this would help. Oh, well, one of these days. At least we have a continuous supply of milk. We can take our time."

Crowbar went back to his digging, and before the sun set he had a trough cut from the stream to the fireplace and back to the stream.

At dawn he was up again, sawing off and carving the wooden boards from the mine shaft so that they would fit into the notches that encircled the outside of the gear. When these paddles were snugly placed he trimmed a long pole to go through the center of the gear, tied a portion of rope around each side so it would not slip off, and carried the wheel to the stream. He carefully anchored the pole and pushed the paddles under one of the waterfalls.

The water fell on the paddles and turned them.

They lifted the water, sped it down the trough to the kitchen and out again.

Returning with fish for breakfast Joe stopped dead in his tracks when he saw it.

"A waterwheel," he gasped.

Crowbar smiled broadly. "Let's just stay here," he said. "We've got everything we need: food, water, beauty. Man, we're crazy to go back to the hassle and frustration of Las Vegas."

"Yeah," said Joe, and for a moment he thought he would stay.

Crowbar opened his arms, fell backward, and splashed into the pool with a cry. "I really like it here, Choe, I really do," he said after surfacing and spurting water high into the air.

When he stood up, Joe answered more practically. "Sure, let's stay here. All we need is a fish market." He held up a few small fish. "Crowbar, we've caught all the big fish. We really need to concentrate on gathering food."

Out of the shelter came Walter, creeping on hands and knees, mouth wide open, eyes wide. He beheld Crowbar's latest creation and crouching before it became so absorbed that he did not feel Joe's arm around him.

"Breakfast is ready," he said, but Walter did not hear.

That morning and the next Joe dug plant roots, picked squash, and milked the burro. If Walter stayed nearby she gave about one cup a day, which they all shared hungrily. If he were not, she gave about three drops. In the afternoons Joe fished and caught lizards and small birds. One night, while seated at the table, he made a pronouncement to Crowbar.

"Our canyon is running out of resources," he said.

"Tomorrow I'm going up on the rim and gather agaves. You've got to help."

Crowbar shrugged, continued his thrashing of some yucca fibers, and silently made a short braid. He placed it in a gourd, filled it with oil he had extracted from several fish, and lit the wick.

A tiny flame danced in the bowl. It played over their faces, casting shadows of their heads like huge ogres on the nearest wall of the canyon.

"Eternal match," he said. "We're getting low on matches."

Walter stared at the lamp, then slipped away. He went back to the waterwheel, watched it for some time, then moved to the plumping mill.

"You may not like what I build," Crowbar said as he took out his knife and began shaping a stick into a dowel for a loom, "but Walter does. He's not running away anymore. He'll stay with us as long as the mill plumps and the waterwheel turns."

"Yeah, but I can't get him to concentrate on his vocabulary," said Joe. "He hasn't learned a durn word practically since you built those things. We're going to die here, Crowbar, unless you help me get food."

"We have milk."

"Don't count on it."

Crowbar put down his knife and shook his stick in Joe's face.

"Listen, I'm getting tired of your damn nagging. I'm keeping us alive with flour and water and all you do is gripe. We don't need to work. All we need to do is teach Walter to fetch."

"Fetch?" said Joe incredulously. "He's no dog. You can't do that."

"I don't know about you," snapped Crowbar, "but I want to live." He stood up. "Walter! Come!"

The boy stared at him blankly, then back at the contraption.

Crowbar walked to the pipe gate of the plumping mill and sticking a stone in front of it, turned it off.

Walter leaped up and hissed like a snake as Crowbar returned. Crowbar hissed back, took a log off the woodpile by the fireplace, and threw it on the ground.

"Fetch," he said, demonstrating, then threw it down again near Walter. "Fetch, and I'll turn on the mill."

Walter grabbed the log and returned it to the fireplace.

"Cook," he enunciated as if to correct Crowbar.

"Fetch!" Crowbar yelled angrily, grabbing the log and throwing it down again. "Pick it up and bring it to me!"

Joe grabbed Crowbar's mouth to stop him from shouting, but it was too late. Walter, confused and frightened, had run up the stream.

"Now, you've done it," snapped Joe. "He says *cook* and you make him fetch. You got to cook when he says *cook*, so he can see what happens when he makes that sound."

"Shut up!" shouted Crowbar.

Above his cry rose a whinny from Walter. It was answered by the mare and the sound of stone poles being scattered. In a few minutes the boys saw Walter lying across the back of the mare as she ran up the mine trail. She slipped, clambered up the last steep slope, and dashed over the rim of the canyon. The foal clattered behind.

"There goes everything," said Joe.

# People

The next day Crowbar arose early and went out to the plumping mill, pulled out the rock, and turned it on.

"*Thump, kerplunk*," the sound echoed around the canyon, a lure for Walter, he hoped. When Walter did not appear, Crowbar tied limbs to each end of the mill and they waved like green signal flags, up and down, up and down.

"That ought to get him," he said with a chuckle.

Joe awoke, stirred up some cattail cakes, baked and ate a few, then went to the stream for a long drink to fill his stomach and stave off the hunger pains. Picking up the grapefruit bag and mayonnaise jar, he set out along the stream.

"Where are you going?"

"Up to the desert to gather agaves," he snapped. "And by the way, stop wasting your time; Walter will be back. He needs us, too."

He strode up the canyon valley without looking back.

The top of the canyon was a sandstone plateau that stretched for many miles toward a series of low walls and terraces. Beyond these, in the blue distance, rose the massive Red Wall into which Havasu Creek, somewhere, cut the canyon valley of the Havasupai people.

But where? Which direction? For a moment he thought about striking out to the northeast . . . but a miscalculation of one step could confound itself into a miss of a hundred miles, and he knew better than to explore.

Instead he concentrated on the tall agave plants that looked like pineapple tops and were sparsely scattered across the landscape. Spotting one that bore fruit (it took a plant ten years to do so), he walked toward it, laying down piles of stone about every twenty paces so that he could find his way back. A shift of light, a pileup of clouds, and the canyon changed its shape and form, and walkers were lost in its undefined space.

The plant Joe selected was on the side of a wash in the stony landscape. Gingerly he approached the cluster of fleshy leaves with their spiked tips and cut down the tall scape. On it hung hundreds of fruits which he stripped and put in the bag. Then he wrapped his shirt around the plant and yanked until it came out of the ground. He would use the fibers to make the hemp string and cord which they always seemed to be needing. A few steps away stood an agave that was about to flower. Joe cut it down the scape and drained the ciderlike juice into the mayonnaise jar. He was starting back when he heard a bray.

A family of burros was coming up the wash. Anxiously he looked among them for Walter, but he was not there, and Joe went on, listening to their hoofbeats and whinnies. Among their sounds he suddenly heard a familiar whinny and he darted to a rise above the wash and looked down on the herd more carefully. Surely he had heard Walter's mare emitting her *hello Walter* sound.

The animals raced to a bend in the cut and there a stallion reared and pawed the air. His family of seven skidded to a stop behind him, their ears twitching in excitement. Once more the mare whinnied her Walter call note and Joe gasped with relief as up and around the bend came Walter, listing slightly to the side, head back, hair flying as he greeted his burro friends.

"Walter!"

He stopped and looked up at Joe. He had heard.

Joe whistled and once more the barrier of silence was broken. Running to meet him, Joe saw that he was carrying a burlap bag. Had he been to the river? He must have. Where else would he find such a thing?

"Choe," said Walter holding out the bag as the burros caught Joe's scent, turned, and went galloping down the draw.

Joe peered into the bag. Inside was a can of beer and a ring-tailed cat. To Joe the dead animal was life itself. Carefully smoked and apportioned, it could last them a week, and give them more time to teach Walter what a village was.

Starting off at a happy trot, Joe looked back over his shoulder and saw the old blank expression on Walter's face. Of course, he had not hugged him. Swinging right around he ran up to the boy, swept him up in his arms, and kissed his dirty cheek. Walter tucked his head in Joe's shoulder and sighed pleasurably.

88

As they walked back toward Canyon Street, Joe poked the little boy affectionately. He smiled. Joe tickled him. Walter burst into his braying laugh, and when Joe stopped, Walter put his hand on his ribs. He looked into Joe's face and opened and closed his mouth.

"Tickle," Joe enunciated carefully.

"Tickle," Walter repeated. He was silent, thinking. "Choe tickle Walter."

"That's right," Joe said. He could hear his voice shaking with the excitement he felt over Walter's discovery of verbs. "Choe tickle Walter again." And he did so, until his pupil was laughing so hard that his eyes watered and he was forced to roll in the grass.

When he finally picked himself up, he reached in the bag and took out the animal. "Fetch," he said proudly. "Walter fetch . . ." He paused.

"Cat," said Joe guiltily. Curse Crowbar. "The name is cat."

"Name," repeated Walter. "Name: cat. . . . Cat," the boy said thoughtfully.

He pointed to the plants in Joe's bag. "Name?"

"Agave."

"Agave." His wide lips pulled back from his teeth, his eyes widened.

"Tarzan, name," he said. Joe nodded vigorously. A window had been cut into the night of Walter's world. He now understood that objects had names which were sounds that represented them, even when they were out of sight. Tarzan was a sound that brought an image to Walter's mind. Joe cheered inside his heart.

They walked slowly back to the top of their canyon. Joe was eager to name everything he saw for the boy: the rocks, the sun, the clouds, the lizards that scurried before them, but he had learned the hard way that he had to be patient. He must let Walter set the pace. Biting his lips to keep himself quiet they arrived at the trail into Inner Kingdom.

"Name," said Walter, shaking the burlap.

"Bag."

"Name," Walter said, pointing to the plumping mill rocking back and forth in the meadow below, limbs flailing and flying like a fan dancer.

"Mill." Joe looked down on the home Crowbar had created: the stone house, the fireplace, the mill, table, and the patch of wild squash. From here it was a village; Crowbar had made a village. Walter was also staring at it. Excitedly Joe realized that if Walter had ever seen Supai, this was the time to teach him *village*. He pointed to Inner Kingdom.

"Village," he said. "The name is village . . . do you know where the village is?"

"Wow-ter," he seemed to mumble as he stared at the mill and house.

Joe snapped his fingers and swore at himself in disgust. Once more he had pushed his student too far and they were back at the beginning. He reached into his bag, took out some fruit, and sat down in the dust.

"Agave," he said, handing one to Walter; then he bit into another. They ate in silence, Joe searching the hot endless waste for even the park helicopter; but they had left the National Park border above Havasu Creek, and only heat mirages moved in the blazing white landscape.

"Wal-ter. Choe, Tarzan," Walter said, tapping Joe's arm. His forehead was wrinkled with thought and perplexity. He wants to know something. He is

90

asking for something . . . a name? A name for all three of us?

"Oh my gosh," he blurted. "People. Walter, Choe, Tarzan, people."

"People," mumbled Walter, nodding his head slowly; then his eyes grew dull and he slipped back into his world, closing a door on vision and windows on sound. They sat quietly in the muted world, mere specks in the abandoned canyon, and yet Joe had hope in his heart.

Presently he arose and led Walter down the wall to the mine trail. As they passed the empty corral and took the turn that led straight to 20 Canyon Street, Joe held high the cat.

"Yo, Crowbar!" he shouted when he saw him near their house, a slab of stone in his hands. One wall of a new building was finished; another was half completed. Crowbar is angry, Joe thought. He is building himself a separate house.

The sight of Walter and the cat, however, brightened Crowbar's sour expression, and he dropped the stone and stumbled to meet them, smiling once more.

"But this isn't the best of our news," Joe said. "Walter knows what people are! Now we can go on to the next lesson. We can teach him *village.*" He turned to show off the boy, but Walter was crouched by the plumping mill watching it fill, dump, and pound.

"He also knows what *fetch* means," said Joe softly. "But we can't abuse it."

Walter turned around. "Fetch," he said clearly. "Tarzan fetch agave." His eyes twinkled.

"You were mentioning abuse?" Crowbar said sourly to Joe. But he looked relieved.

"Fetch!" Walter shouted. "Choe fetch Walter-bag."

"Hey, enough of that," said Joe. But he picked up the burlap bag and obediently handed it over.

Reaching in under the cat, Walter pulled out a pair of radio headphones he had found apparently in the river.

"Name?" he asked.

"Earphones," shouted Crowbar and turned to Joe. "Explain *that* word to him?"

They laughed together for the first time in many hours. Joe slapped Crowbar on the shoulders and picked the cat out of the bag to skin and prepare for smoking.

"Earphones!" Crowbar spun around. "My gosh, do you know what that means?"

"No, what?" said Joe.

"It means we can make a radio. There's some copper wire up in the mine and . . . quartz crystals — great big, huge crystals."

"So?"

"That's all you need for a simple receiver."

"And where's the electricity?"

"Don't need it. The crystal and cooper wire rolled make a magnetic field. They pick up radio waves. Those earphones will amplify them. Wow! Man, Joe, think of it. We can sit down here and listen to music and the news; we can hear the Outer Kingdom again."

Crowbar shouted excitedly and ran up the path to the mine. Joe sighed and placed the cat on the kitchen table. "There he goes again," he said to himself. "Gets a little food in the larder, and he starts playing."

Walter went back to the plumbing mill, put a stone in the pipe, and observed that the water stopped flowing and the mill stopped running. He took it out and the water flowed again and the mill went up and down. Over and over he repeated the experiment; then he moved to the waterwheel and watched it. Joe built a smoking rack, skinned the cat, and cut the meat into strips.

The evening meal of squash and agaves, washed down with agave cider, pepped up the boys and they began to hum and sing. Walter helped Joe wash the stone plates by turning on the waterwheel, following the water down the millrace to the pool in the kitchen, and then scrubbing the gourds and wooden forks.

Well fed, they all sat happily around the table and watched Crowbar's agile fingers scrape the oxide off the copper wire and wrap it around a roll of bark. He grounded one end of the coiled wire, then carefully mounted a crystal between two short wires and twisted them together at each end. One of these ends he fastened to one of the two wires from the earphones.

"I need a piece of flat metal," he said. "Little piece."

"Walter found a can of beer. Will that do?"

"Yeah, the pop top; that would be perfect." Joe got the can and opened it. He handed the pop top to Crowbar.

"Want the beer?" he asked; but Walter reached out and took it. Gulping and slurping he emptied the can, wiped his mouth, and stared down at Crowbar's hands.

"Well, he knows what beer's all about," said Crowbar with a chuckle; then he looked up at Walter. "The name is beer."

"Beer," said Walter as a long burp rolled out of his belly. He smiled and pointed to Crowbar's contraption.

"Name," he asked.

93

"Radio, we hope," said Joe.

"Radio, we hope," mumbled Walter.

Crowbar fastened the other end of the wires that surrounded the crystal to the pop top, then stretched an antenna of copper wire from the crystal to the nearest cottonwood. He attached the second wire on the earphones to the ground wire, placed the earphones over his head and slowly moved the pop top along the coil.

"Stations are on this coil. I should pick one up with this pop top."

Joe waited in fascination, studying Crowbar's face. Suddenly it lit up.

"Static, Joe. . . . We're getting static. Wow! Listen."

He handed him the earphones and Joe too listened to the crackling and screeching that came in through the tuner and crystal. He shook his head, grinned in amazement, and put them on Walter's head. As the sounds came to Walter he looked up wide-eyed at the sky, then under the table. Finally he took off the earphones and poked his finger into the amplifier.

"Name," he cried in delight.

"Static," answered Crowbar and he put on the earphones to search for a voice or some music.

Crowbar sat up late with his gadget and failed to awake at dawn, so Joe got up, took the fishnet and went seining alone. He caught a few small fish, dug some of the last of the cattail tubers, and stopped by the corral to repair it in hopes that the bighorn sheep would come down for water and get caught.

Returning to the kitchen in the late afternoon, he found Walter playing with the mill and Crowbar hunched over the radio.

"Meager pickings," said Joe, throwing down the bag.

"I've got a country music station somewhere in Utah," Crowbar said. "Listen." He took off the earphones and handed them to Joe.

"I'm not going to listen. I think you've gone nuts. We've *all* got to help find food."

"Why should *I* when Walter's so much better at it?" Crowbar asked with a sneer. "Walter," he called. The boy took the stone plug out of the end of the pipe and watched the water flow for the hundredth time.

"Walter fetch agaves," Crowbar commanded. Walter did not move and Crowbar walked over to him and put his foot on the plug end of the pipe to prevent him from working the plumping mill.

Walter dug the mud under the stone plug and tried to pull it from under his foot. Crowbar held it down with both feet.

"Fetch agave," he said. "Then you can play with the mill."

"Walter fetch agave," the boy said softly, picked up the burlap bag and, loping up the trail, scaled the wall, and disappeared over the rim.

"I don't like this, Crowbar. I don't like this at all." Joe spun on his heel and went off to gather watercress. Crowbar grinned and sat down at the table. Once more he put on the earphones.

Walter did not return at sundown, and Joe and Crowbar sat in silence, no longer speaking. When Crowbar at last stopped tinkering with the radio, the stars had been out for hours. He stood up to go to bed.

"Walter's a person, Crowbar," snapped Joe. "You can't send him out to fetch. That's slavery."

"It's slavery to you when you're full. It's survival when you're hungry. For me it's survival all the time so I'm going to send him out."

Crowbar stared Joe in the eyes.

"You've become a durn saintly lecturer now that you think you're a teacher." He turned on his heel. "Tonight I am sleeping in my own house."

Joe listened as Crowbar stumped off to bed; then he sat down at the table and dropped his head in his hands.

"I think we're going to have a war and die in this place," he said.

# Village

Walter did not come to breakfast. Crowbar ate and went back to work on the radio. Joe picked up the net and went seining for fish again. At noon he returned, cleaned and cooked the meager catch, and served it for lunch on watercress with stewed monkey flower leaves.

After cleaning up the fireplace and stone dishes he went foraging on the plateau again, his eyes scanning for sight of Walter. Returning to the kitchen with a bag of agave, he stood before the waterwheel and watched it uselessly pump water down the millstream and past the fireplace.

"We're beginning to have a food shortage in this little canyon," he said to Crowbar, who was cleaning the millstream. "We're eating ourselves out of house and home. We'll have to take longer and longer trips into the desert for agaves."

"Okay," said Crowbar. He stomped off, put on the earphones, and began touching each coil of wire with the pop top. Presently Crowbar took off the earphones.

"You'd be less hungry if you sat still or slept more," he said, then added, "I think I've got a couple of men on walkie-talkies here. Sounds like they're down on the river or something."

"Fascinating," said Joe and sat down to sort the food. He went to bed without speaking to Crowbar.

Sometime during the night the leaves in Walter's bed rattled, awakening Joe. He sleepily looked toward the door and saw the fuzzy head of the boy silhouetted against the starry sky. Joe watched him pack down the leaves and finally curl up. A deep sigh said that he was home at last. Walter's progress out of the darkness of silence began, Joe recalled, with a good sincere hug, but had spurted along when the boy had moved into the shelter, accepting and imitating new ways.

In the morning Joe was cleaning squash when Walter came to the kitchen and sat down at the table.

"Name," he said and Joe turned to see what he had now. There on the table sat the blue urn with the silver top.

"My God, Crowbar," he yelled.

"My God, Crowbar," repeated Walter and turned over in his hands the wondrous thing that had such a long name.

Crowbar sat up in his house, saw the urn and bolted to the scene without bothering to pull on his jeans.

"My God, Crowbar," said Walter, holding up the pretty object and smiling. Crowbar grabbed the urn and opened it.

"Empty," he said.

"Maybe Walter dumped old Roland out," sur-

98

mised Joe. "Anyway we've got another water jar for the exodus."

"People," said Walter. "People. Bang, bang, kersplat."

The boy opened the urn, stuck his hand inside and clutching something imaginary in it, took it out, and bent over it. He then threw the urn away. Listing with great exaggeration, he crossed the meadow and picked it up.

"People fetch Walter." He grabbed his own arm, fought an imaginary enemy, then ran. Returning to the kitchen he said, "People, bang, bang, kersplat!"

"Wow, someone's been shooting at him."

"And someone took something out of the urn." Crowbar put the earphones on and pinpointed the walkie-talkie.

Walter pointed toward the mouth of the canyon. The ravens soared in the distance as if following something.

"People, people," he said and made running motions in place.

"Someone is after him," yelled Joe. "Let's get out of here."

Crowbar took the earphones off and handed them to Joe.

"I got the walkie-talkie. See what you make of it."

Joe put on the earphones. Through the screeches and crackles came a man's voice.

"Where did he go?" Did you see?"

"Roger, up that draw." *Crackle, snap.*

"Does he still have the urn?"

"Roger." Pause and screeches. "Como will have our hides for this, a kid stealing the pay dirt."

Joe's heart thumped. Como was not an ordinary name. *Pay dirt*, what was that?

"You sure he's alive? I thought I saw Roy shoot him."

"Roy missed. Get up here. I see a cave. He must be in it."

Joe took off the earphones and stared at Walter. He pushed a stone across the table and followed it with another.

"Follow; this stone is following that one. People follow Walter?" he asked.

Walter nodded, but sensing the distress in Joe and Crowbar he was now nodding at everything. Joe turned to Crowbar.

"Did you hear anything about money on that crystal set?" he asked. He was too perplexed and upset to mention that he had heard the name Como.

"Well not exactly, but one guy mentioned Roland."

"Wow, I heard money."

"Well, we never opened the urn," said Crowbar. "Could be Roland was money."

"Mmmm," mumbled Joe. "So that's why we were told definitely not to open the urn . . . not to scatter. Durn! Something's rotten here."

"Maybe," said Crowbar. "But Uncle Como wouldn't get us into anything like this."

"I hope not," Joe replied and put on the earphones, listened for a moment, and then removed them. "I got a copter pilot," he said. "He is headed for Peach Springs. He said: 'Barley, this is Scott. I'm coming in with Roland.' . . . And the walkie-talkie guys think Walter has Roland.

"Let's get out of here."

Snatching up the grapefruit bag, he threw in the remainder of the smoked meat, cattail tubers, agaves, and squash.

Crowbar filled the mayonnaise jar and urn with water, tied them together, and slung them over his shoulder. He grabbed the raft rope, the matches, and his knife, then looked around at Inner Kingdom.

"I'll be back," he whispered.

Hollow voices, seemingly coming from the soulless rocks, rose on the heat waves. The boys turned and ran. Walter ran, too.

At the top of the canyon Crowbar looked back at Inner Kingdom. He blew a kiss to the plumping mill, waterwheel, and little stone houses. The smoke from the dying fire rose in a puff, then reaching the hot air above the cool canyon floor, spiraled into the sky.

Walter stared at the smoke.

"Village," he said, turning to Joe. "Village?" he asked pointing down at their home.

"Yes, village. That's a village," Joe shouted. He pushed the dusty hair from Walter's face and concentrated on holding his attention. "Walter fetch Choe and Tarzan to village."

The boy's eyes dimmed, then brightened again.

"Village," he whispered, and holding his hands together began to spread them apart.

Joe watched him, knowing he wanted a word, trying to guess it. What is he doing? Think, Joe think, he said to himself. This is your chance. What does he want?

"What word does he need, Crowbar?" he asked, biting a nail. "We're close, so close to being saved."

The hands moved out, expanding the distance between them like a fisherman's description of his fish.

"Walter fetch Choe, Tarzan to . . ." The boy's lips opened, waiting for the word.

"Big!" shouted Joe. "Big village. Yes, yes, that's it, he knows Supai!"

101

"Walter fetch Choe, Tarzan to big village," Walter said, then pointing down to Inner Kingdom added: "Name . . . ?"

"Little village."

"Okay," he said, eyes bright with understanding, "Walter fetch Choe and Tarzan to big village." Listing to the side, he bowed his head in the hot sun and started off across the blazing plateau.

"Fetch to big village," he repeated over and over again, laughing happily every time he turned around and saw that Joe and Crowbar were following. He was alive with excitement. He had understood words and could help his friends.

At long last he was awake.

At the far edge of the lava flow, Walter walked up a side canyon that twisted south, then led to the top of a mesa. Presently the land flattened. They were on the Tonto Platform.

"We're going to live," Joe shouted, looking down. "We're going to live. We're on the trail to Supai village." Walter darted forward.

The sun hammered their heads and skin and dried their tongues, but with red limestone under their feet, Joe knew they were only a few miles from help. He ran to catch up with Walter and, putting his arm around his shoulder, walked and whistled in the blasting heat.

# Supai

Supai village lay in a jade green meadow cut into the Red Wall by Havasu Creek. The valley was pear-shaped, wide at the upper end and tapering as the stream cascaded, then dropped two hundred feet before racing off to the Colorado. On the far side of the village stood three huge limestone pillars carved into giants by the prehistoric wanderings of the creek.

Small one-room houses, each beside a patch of vegetable garden, were clustered around the dirt crossroad in the center of town. At the quiet intersection stood the grocery store–post office. No automobiles came into Supai; the road down from the South Rim was traveled only by foot and horse. Supplies were brought into town twice a week by a pack train that wound down the dusty switchbacks.

Fine horses, the pride of the Havasupai men, tossed their manes and pawed the ground in well-kept stables near the houses. In the cool of evening their owners raced them down the main street of town, a wide avenue of red clay shaded by mammoth ancient cottonwoods. Burros in makeshift corrals slept or munched grass while chickens beneath them snatched the grass seeds even as they chewed.

Strands of smoke curled up from fireplaces in front of several houses, for it was late afternoon and some of the three hundred villagers were starting their fires in preparation for the evening meal. On tree limbs nearby hung pots and pans, saddles, boots, and utensils. The villagers lived outdoors; their houses were merely bedrooms and shelters from occasional rains and cold spells.

Bright blue-green Havasu Creek was the centerpiece of the village. Colored by the minerals it leeched out of the canyon rocks, the beautiful fifteen-foot-wide stream romped through town, cut across the fields, and thundered over famous Mooney Falls, causing clouds and windstorms at the bottom.

Along its course the creek irrigated large communal fields of alfalfa and corn as well as melon patches, peach and fig trees, and the watering holes of the community's beef cattle. The stream made life possible in the canyon, and because of it the Indians called themselves the Havasupai, "peoples of the blue-green waters."

The wind blew along the high cliff where the boys lay on their stomachs, spotting the Bureau of Indian Affairs school and the home of the chairman of the tribal council — a larger house than the others with three splendid black horses in the corral. At Walter's urging, Joe taught him the word *house*. The Mormon church was easy to recognize, the hotel and movie house less so; but it was the telephone wire that came down from the Rim that interested Joe. It led to the store.

"I see why Walter finally remembered what village meant from looking down on Inner Kingdom. It's amazing how much our houses, corral, and outdoor fireplace look like theirs." He stood up, stretched, and turned to Crowbar. "You did good, Crowbar. It was you who made our village." He grabbed his hand and shook it. "And now for the jackpot question. . . . What are we going to do with Walter?"

"Aren't we going to take him to Las Vegas? He'll want to be with us. We're the only ones who can understand him."

"I can see us now, taking him to school and walking into Mrs. Pawley's room. I'd say, 'Mrs. Pawley, I want you to meet my friend Walter. He eats lizards and wants to learn.' "

"Ho," roared Crowbar. "She'd faint right on the spot." He looked at Walter's calloused body and the sprigs of grass in his hair. "Then she'd lock him up in an institution. Yeah, we can't do that."

"She thinks we need psychiatrists," said Joe. "Wonder what she'd prescribe for Walter." They chuckled at the thought of Mrs. Pawley's first sight of their untamed friend.

"He could stay at my house," suggested Crowbar. "My brother's gone. We've got an extra room."

"Crowbar, your mom would have him by the hair, scrubbed, and packed off to school so fast he'd think he was riding a thunderbolt."

"Ooooh, true, true." Crowbar poked a finger in one of many holes in his battered sneakers, glad they were still a protection. "What *do* we do with him?"

"Maybe we should try to ask him what he'd like to do. We could try to get across some kind of choice to him. He could go back to the river . . . or . . . maybe the Indian school here would consider helping him. We should speak to the chairman of the tribal council."

"Yeah, we should ask Walter. He just might want to go back and live in Inner Kingdom. He can catch fish and watch the plumping mill. We could come visit him, too. I'd like that." Crowbar paused, his brow knitting thoughtfully. "I don't think he ought to be in a town, any town. He's beautiful as he is: wild and free."

"But he hasn't really been free since we taught him to talk again," said Joe. "He wants things now . . . friends."

"Yeah," agreed Crowbar. "But they'll never appreciate him, especially the white teachers at the Bureau of Indian Affairs. They'll think he's dumb because he doesn't know about clothes and books or even saddles and boots. They won't know he can snag ravens on the wing, catch lizards, or maneuver the rapids like a fish."

Walter was lying on his back staring at a distant horizon. Slowly he pulled himself into a sitting position and concentrated his attention on a blue-purple cloud coming their way.

"Name," he said to Joe, who turned and saw that half the sky was black and spiked with dazzling lightning bolts.

"Thunderstorm," he answered. Now on his feet, Walter pointed to his mouth, then hopped from foot to foot in frustration.

"He wants to tell us something," said Crowbar.

A powerful wind picked up dust and pebbles and hurled them like darts. Joe and Crowbar ducked to get beneath the assault while Walter danced and shook his fists. A bolt of lightning rolled across the plateau, leaped to a pinnacle, and exploded with a blinding flash.

"Thunderstorm . . . house," bleated Walter, then struck himself on the chest and dropped to the ground. He lay still.

"I think he's trying to tell us to get out of here; that this storm is a killer."

Joe grabbed the food bag. Crowbar picked up the rope and water sling, and they climbed over the rim and down the wall. Suddenly the sun was blotted out and the cliffside trembled under the constant thunder roll. The boys pressed against the cliff, edging down toward the trees as the storm roared overhead, sounding like the inside of Lava Falls.

Down in the willows at the bottom of the cliff, Joe looked around for a ledge to get under. As the air crackled, all the hairs on his body rose on end. He looked up. The entire plateau was a sizzling electrical charge.

"Good old Walter," he said. The rain began, and spotting a cave up on the ledge he headed toward it, but Walter grabbed his foot and hung on.

"No, Choe, no," he cried.

Now trusting the boy's wisdom, Joe turned. Walter pulled him down into the willow grove, lashed a group of young saplings together with the rope, and in the splattering rain, wove branches in and out. Then he crawled in. Joe and Crowbar followed him into a sapling tepee.

The dark cloud opened and a river of water dropped from the sky. Walter huddled between Joe and Crowbar, his eyes lifted toward the fire and thunder above. Joe's eyes followed his. Suddenly a bolt struck the cave where Joe would have crawled and burned the rocks black. Joe saw it come alive with fire and he hugged Walter gratefully.

"Thanks, fellow."

Then almost as suddenly as the storm had come, it ended. The sun came out, the air was crisp and clean, and the purple cloud rumbled off to the river. Joe stuck his head out of the tepee and looked around. Cascades tumbled in solid white veils down all the walls, making the canyon one vast silver waterfall that sparkled in the sun.

Joe gasped at its beauty; then opening his water-proof match case, saw the ten dollars he had put there at the beginning of the trip. It was time to use it.

Streams of water ran across the floor of the tepee as the rain poured off the plateau. Finally they trickled and came to a stop. Joe walked out into the sun. "Let's leave Walter here," he suggested, "while we call Uncle Como and then speak to the chairman."

Crowbar nodded. "*We* look enough like river rats," he said.

Pressing down his hair, he tied a string around his head to keep it in place and told Joe to tuck his ragged T-shirt into his blue jeans. As presentable as they could make themselves, they started through the willow grove.

"Walter, Walter," the boy screamed, darting from the shelter and seizing Joe's hand. For a moment Joe hesitated. It would be easier to explain Walter if he did not come with them; but the boy's eyes were hurt and so terrified that he changed his mind.

Crossing his arms, Joe pulled his shirt over his head, held it up for a moment, then slipped it on Walter.

"Now, you're ready for the village," he said.

Walter stood transfixed, looking down at the

muddy rag that hung from his shoulders to his knees. Slowly he lifted his head and smiled.

"You look real good," said Crowbar. "You're a real clotheshorse."

"Choe, Tarzan, Walter," he said loudly and held on to their hands until they reached a horse trail in the willow grove. Then, in single file, they followed the path around a field to a wide clay road that led to the grocery store–post office.

The residents of the houses along the way had retreated into their homes when the storm struck and most were still inside. Only a child or two, splashing in the enormous red puddles, saw the strange threesome walking down the road. But muddy tourists from the river came to Supai often in the summer and children paid no attention. They went on laughing and kicking up the water.

At the grocery store only the clerk sat at the counter. The people who had run there for shelter during the storm were now racing to their animals to dry them and to their gardens to dam up the water and save it.

The three boys stepped into the dark store. Suddenly Joe's mouth watered. Food was everywhere. He took down from a shelf a large jar of peanut butter, several cans of tuna fish, a loaf of bread, and a bag of potato chips. Crowbar picked up a quart of milk. Joe paid for the groceries and with the change, stepped to the telephone on the wall and dialed Uncle Como.

"Who's this?" he barked, and although he sounded angry, Joe realized for the first time how homesick he was.

"It's me, Joe," he said, his voice breaking.

"Joe? You're kidding. Where are you?"

"Supai village," he shouted happily. "I'm okay, so is Crowbar. Call Mom and Mrs. Flood."

"Do you have the urn?"

"Well, yes. . . ." He was disappointed that his uncle did not ask how they were, say he was happy that he was alive.

"Wait there," he shouted. "Don't move. It'll take me about four or five hours to reach the trail and several to ride a horse down. I'll see you about dawn. Don't go away."

He hung up. Joe turned and slowly walked to Crowbar, who saw the disillusionment on his friend's face.

"What's wrong?" he asked.

"He seemed angry," Joe said.

"Well, we did mess something up, I guess. Roland and all that helicopter stuff."

"What *did* we mess up?" Joe asked as he opened the potato chips.

Crowbar reached in for a handful and Joe looked for Walter. His head was tilted upward, nostrils moving as he followed the scent of chocolate right to the candy counter.

"Oh, my gosh," Joe said, grabbing his hand and pulling him away. "Let's get him out of here. They won't appreciate his genius."

Turning back for a handful of candy bars, he paid for them and, holding one in front of Walter's nose, lured him out of the store.

"The chairman of the tribal council lives over there under the big cottonwood," said Crowbar, pointing. "Shall we go?"

"Not now." Walter had caught the scent of peaches and leaped into the limb of a tree in a garden. Swinging over the branches he filled his shirt and dropped lightly to the ground.

110

"No, peaches!" Joe scolded, took them away from him and placed them on the ground. Opening the peanut butter jar he gave Walter a taste. His face lit up and when he plunged for more, Joe, holding the jar high, ran all the way back to their shelter.

Inside the steamy structure, now drying in the hot sun, Crowbar and Joe made peanut butter sandwiches as fast as they could. Walter ate until his stomach was round. After he washed down the sandwiches with milk, they fed him a whole can of tuna fish. Walter rolled over on his side and closed his eyes. So full and content was he that even the smell of meat cooking on the open fireplaces in the village did not interest him.

Joe and Crowbar sighed and ate their share of peanut butter and tuna. They wondered what to do next, but night came quickly, and before they could come to any conclusions they were all fast asleep.

Around four-thirty in the morning, as the stars were fading, Joe was awakened by a soft voice.

"Boy, boy." He sat up. A little girl was peering through the willow stems.

"There's a man to see you," she said. Joe rolled to his knees and looked into her round black eyes.

"How did you know we were here?"

"I saw you yesterday at father's store. You had Nag Noo Chee . . . the wild boy."

"You know him?"

"A little. . . . Sometimes I see him. Always alone. You are his first friends. He would not play with me. But once he watched me spin yucca."

Her eyes widened when she saw Walter sleeping, but before she could say any more Uncle Como had pulled back the willows and wedged his shoulder into the shelter.

111

"Where's the urn?"

The little girl, frightened by the force of his voice, turned and ran away.

"Right here," said Joe, rising sleepily. For a moment he stood with his back to his uncle, wondering what to do. Then he reached behind Walter and picked up the blue urn.

"Roland is hard to lose," he said, passing it to him. "We dumped him but he came swirling back on an eddy. We wrecked in Lava Falls."

Uncle Como was not interested. He grabbed the urn, spun the silver lid, and opened it. Water slopped over his pants and feet.

"Where's the money?" he snarled.

"What money?"

He grabbed and shook Joe until he thought his neck would snap.

"I didn't see any money. We dumped the urn without opening it; just like you said."

Uncle Como shook him again.

"When we got it from the river about two weeks later, it was empty. That's all I know."

Crowbar was now on his knees staring at the enraged man.

"What was in it, Uncle Como?" Crowbar asked.

"A fortune, that's what. . . . A fortune in cash. The syndicate hires me to pass money."

Shaking Joe once more, he grabbed him under the armpit and pulled him close to his face.

"You are lying. I know you are. What did you do with the money?"

"Nothing! It was empty when we found it. It was."

Uncle Como glanced at Walter, who was now standing, and pulled him up to his face with his other hand.

"Who's this kid?" He shook him. "You, what did *you* do with the money?"

Walter's eyes filmed over and he gazed up at Uncle Como without seeing. His cheeks turned gray and his mouth fell open.

"*Hey, you,*" shouted Uncle Como. He let go of Joe and poked his fingers at Walter's eyes.

"What is he? An idiot? You got an idiot with you?" He thrust the boy to the ground.

"Quit that." Joe stepped between Walter and his uncle. "If you calm down I'll tell you something."

His uncle grabbed him under the armpit again.

"Speak or I'll shake your teeth out."

"I'm not going to talk till you stop," said Joe, surprised at his own courage.

"There was a quarter of a million in that jug, Joe. Where is it? The switchmen radioed me that they got to Eddy 202, where all the stuff from Lava Falls catches, just as some kid picked it up and ran off with it. That must have been you!" He shook him again.

Joe pinched his lips together and stared into his uncle's bloodshot eyes.

"I'm not talking to you when you're like this."

"Be careful, Joe," Crowbar warned. "Don't talk back. He's crazy mad."

Joe folded his hand quietly on his chest and stared at his uncle.

"I'll tell you something when you're calm," he persisted.

"Talk." Uncle Como raised his fist.

Joe did not speak.

"Okay, okay, Josie," said his uncle, taking another tack. "I'm just kidding. What do you know?"

"This is a complicated story and I'm not going into the details, but Crowbar made a crystal radio set in the canyon where we were marooned for a long time.

"I put on the earphones and happened to get the pilot of a helicopter headed for Peach Springs. This is what he said to someone waiting for him: 'Barley, this is Scott. I'm coming in with Roland.'"

Uncle Como's face lost all expression, his lower eyelids drooped, his cheeks sagged.

"Barley and Scott. Barley in a copter? He got there first in a copter?" He whistled and wiped the perspiration from his forehead.

"Barley and Scott." Uncle Como swore for a full minute, then looked at Joe. "Thank you very much, Josie. Thanks, Crowbar. I know who's got the dough. I think I'll be off to Mexico. Thanks for the tip."

Uncle Como turned and ran, but at the edge of the willow grove he stopped.

"Joe," he called. "Your mother and Mrs. Flood are waiting for you at the top of Havasu Trail. They'll be real glad to see you. Real glad."

"Wow, Crowbar, hear that!" exclaimed Joe. "Mom's going to be real glad to see me. My mom's waiting at the top of the trail."

Uncle Como's horse whinnied; then its feet struck the earth and he galloped down the trail and out of earshot.

Joe shook his head and looked up at Crowbar.

"I'm sorry," he said. "Some job I got you into."

"Not your fault."

"I really thought Uncle Como was okay."

"Oh, he's okay. He's just in a mess. Lots of people get into messes." Crowbar put his arm around Joe's shoulders.

114

"Yeah," Joe said and glanced at the stony Walter, who was in his world of no world, cold and frightened. The three sat in silence until the sun came up. Finally Joe spoke to Crowbar.

"We've still got the important job to do," he said, unwrapped a chocolate bar and placed it near the withdrawn boy.

"Let's go," said Crowbar. They strode out of the grove and down the road to meet the chairman of the tribal council.

After knocking on Bufford Pata's door they had only to wait a moment before a warm voice called out and a large robust man appeared. He wore blue jeans, a gray shirt, and a yellow and red vest. Around his hair was a yellow band, and rings of turquoise covered his fingers. His broad face and long nose gave him the appearance of a hardy, but noble bear.

Joe introduced Crowbar and himself, and then got down to the business they had come about.

"We have been lost in the canyon for a long time," Joe began, "and we would have died if a wild boy hadn't found us. He saved our lives."

"Wild boy? Yes. I know about him. Yes."

"You do know him?"

"Yes, he's been seen in these parts. But he's deaf and mute and no one can catch him. Wild as an animal."

"Well, he isn't a deaf mute. We have taught him a few words."

Pata's eyebrows went up.

"You have?"

"We are his friends," said Crowbar.

"Friends?"

"Now that he has found friends, he needs others,"

Joe went on. "He wants to be with people and learn. Can he go to school here?"

"No, no." The man shook his long black hair and his face grew firm. "That's not possible. This boy has lived wild in the canyon too long. He was beaten. Ran away from his parents when they were stopped up on the Rim in a camper. They hunted him for one day, then left. I don't know who they are; all I know is that he lived off our gardens for a while and then moved to the river. Now he's an animal, afraid of all people. No, no, we cannot have him."

"But sir," persisted Joe. "He's really smart. He knows so much. He could be of help to you."

"No, no." His voice rose and his wife, who had been standing behind him and had overheard everything, stepped out of the house and crossed the road to a smaller house. Presently she returned with a young woman with straight brown hair and a severely angular face.

"Good day, Bufford Pata," the young woman said. "Mrs. Pata thinks I might help these boys?"

"It's about the wild boy," Bufford Pata said with a sigh. "They want us to take him in. Put him in school." He laughed.

"But he's an idiot," she said, turning to Joe. "He cannot learn."

"No, no, he's real bright; knows everything about the river and canyon; and he can talk now. He's learning new words all the time."

"Talk? Incredible, that's incredible." She questioned Joe and Crowbar further and then turned to Bufford Pata.

"Why don't I examine this boy," she said. "This is a most interesting case. If this is true perhaps he could live with me and Mark. I could study how a

116

child learns. It might be a very valuable study, even a master's thesis."

"I tell you what, Mrs. Hatfield," Bufford Pata said seriously. "I want proof he's not an animal. If these boys can get him here, maybe we'll take him. I know him well. He'll never come." He smiled wisely.

Joe did not wait to hear more.

"Sir, thank you," he said. "We'll be right back. Come on, Crowbar."

Spinning around, the two boys ran all the way back to the shelter. Walter was not there. The chocolate bar was eaten, the peanut butter gone . . . and the blue urn was smashed to pieces . . . deliberately.

"I guess I can understand those words," said Joe quietly. "Walter just said: 'I hate you and all people and I'll never be back.' "

"Yeah," agreed Crowbar. "Uncle Como sure did a job on him."

Joe slung the food bag over his shoulder and Crowbar picked up the mayonnaise jar and the rope "for old times' sake," he said. Slowly they stepped onto the path and walked down the road to the chairman's house. Mrs. Hatfield and Bufford Pata were waiting at a table in the yard. As Mrs. Hatfield rose to meet the boys, the wind twisted strands of hair across her face, softening her stern features.

"I think Walter might have come to like her," Joe whispered to Crowbar.

As they came down the path from the gate, Bufford Pata swung around in his seat and greeted them, then peered down the road with satisfaction.

"No wild boy, huh?"

"Guess you're right, Mr. Pata," Joe answered in a low voice. "He ran away. He won't come in."

117

"I told you. But don't be upset. He's no more than an animal. If he had any real human feelings, he'd be here right now." He nodded knowingly. "He'd have stuck with you."

"Well I'm not sure about that; but maybe it's just as well he stays out. He'll always be a wild boy who rides the river, runs the ledges, and catches fish and lizards. I'd sort of like to remember him that way."

As Joe backed off from the gathering at the table, Mrs. Hatfield's eyes suddenly shone with such tenderness that he actually thought her beautiful. He spun around to see what she was looking at.

Walter stood at the gate, listing to one side, his deepset eyes cast down. His hair was plastered to his head with water and around his T-shirt he had tied a length of yucca cord.

"Walter, Choe, Tarzan," he whispered almost inaudibly.

Joe hurried to him. "Meet your new friends, Walter," he said. "This is Bufford Pata and this is Mrs. Hatfield."

Walter's eyes shifted swiftly from Joe's face to the chairman's and then to the young woman's. She smiled and stepped toward him, her face soft with understanding. Carefully she took Walter's hand in her own and brought it up under her chin. He drew back, but whined pleasantly.

"He's going to be just fine, Bufford Pata," she said, and slipping her arm around Walter's shoulder urged him gently toward her home.

Out on the road he hesitated and looked back at Joe and Crowbar. Mrs. Hatfield encouraged him on a few more steps. He paused once more. This time he glaced swiftly around. He located a little footpath that led off into the canyon and studied it for a long moment. Then he lowered his head and permitted Mrs. Hatfield to nudge him across the dusty road.

"He likes chocolates," Crowbar called, his voice low.

Joe spun on his heel and dashed up the trail before anyone could see the tears that were burning his eyes.

## About the author

Jean Craighead George was born in Washington, D.C., and spent weekends along the Potomac River with her father and brothers learning to canoe, fish, and swim. Their father taught them about plants and animals and how to make a meal off the land.

At age eight, Jean Craighead George knew she wanted to be a writer. Her third grade teacher sent her to the blackboard to solve an arithmetic problem, and finding herself with chalk in hand but no solution to the problem, she instead composed a short poem. Luckily, her teacher congratulated her on the poem, and she has been writing ever since.

Ms. George has three grown children, Twig, Craig, and Luke, and has always kept a variety of wild animals. Like the characters in *River Rats, Inc.*, she has floated down the Grand Canyon of Colorado, and even gone for a swim in one of the rapids.

Currently, Ms. George lives in Chappaqua, N.Y., where she continues to learn and to write about man and nature. She has won the Newbery Medal for her novel, *Julie of the Wolves*.